THE EMPTY BOULEVARDS

A collection of short stories by

WILLIS GORDON

authorHOUSE®

AuthorHouse™
1663 Liberty Drive
Bloomington, IN 47403
www.authorhouse.com
Phone: 1-800-839-8640

Published by AuthorHouse 07/27/2012

ISBN: 978-1-4772-5378-6 (sc)
ISBN: 978-1-4772-5377-9 (e)

Library of Congress Control Number: 2012913730

Contents

Demons

*We give ourselves to God when the
Devil no longer wants us.*

I hate Sunday nights. The dark, quiet, restrained nature they have, the impending doom of work the next morning. After letting you run free for two whole days, you are once again subjected to the chains of the 9-5. A grueling, soul-crushing, fruitless ritual we do to gain power, and social status. Do a good enough job to earn a good enough paycheck to buy a good enough car to catch a good enough woman to have good enough sex and have good enough children and have a good enough life, until you die under the eerie discomfort of dull fluorescent lighting and some temp on the graveyard shift dumps your body in the morgue to the shattering sound of no one caring.

But what do I know? I haven't been to work in a month. They've probably found a replacement by now, some worm to do the bitch work for them. It doesn't matter who does it, we're all faceless to them…

Some folks get off on the power, flexing at other people. Making them feel weak and helpless. I knew an executive once who used to hire secretaries just to berate, belittle, and occasionally cop a feel, which led to tears and subsequent humiliation. After he fired them for being "Weak" and "Without vision" he'd be in a good mood for the rest of the week.

We all have our kinks and our vices. We gotta get off somehow. For the past 4 weeks I was holed up in my filthy apartment with endless bottles of cheap beer and rot-gut

My hands are bleeding. I must've tripped in the gravel. I don't even remember it. I'm running now, harder and with more abandon than ever. *But where am I going?* I look around. *I'm trying to get to 12th street so I can catch a cab... Get to the train station. She-* **We** *owe the dope man money.* Have to get to 12th. I must've run right into the storm, it's raining hard now. *Christ, it's raining. I'm nearly blind.*

I wave down a taxi on 12th and sling my bag into the cavernous backseat of the Crown Vic before spilling into it myself. I croak out my destination and the Cabbie cranks the windshield wipers into high gear and takes off. He's telling me some story about a customer who called for a pickup and was dissatisfied by the hygiene of the taxi. Or something, I wasn't really listening. Anyone who has ridden in a cab before knows the driver has a running monologue that goes on whether someone is in the back or not.

Hands shaking, I lit a cigarette and slipped the lighter back into my jeans. I heard more musings on the divide between the haves and have-nots in America. Crazy bastard was still going. I took a long, deep drag as I saw the station come into view. We rolled in and he wrapped up, giving me some indistinct, formless moral to it all, and I mumbled my agreement. I gave him the last of the crumpled up bills in my wallet and walked away from my home forever.

I've been on this train for a day and a half now. I used my emergency cash and bought a ticket for the furthest thing headed west. I'm trying to start again, trying to forget the emptiness and Pain I feel whenever I think about her. Whenever I see her face. When I pulled out of the station that stormy Thursday, I watched the raindrops slide down the window. The paths they left looking like wasting veins, track marks. I have to shake that off now, start again. There's still time.

We all have our kinks, our vices...our demons. I know

I have problems to work out, hills to climb; but you know what? So do you. I'm not saying that I'm running off to join the clergy and teach special Ed, because people never change the big things, but I *can* make adjustments. I know it. I have to believe it.

There's still time.

Peace in the Valley

*"I'm ten years burning down the road,
nowhere to run, nowhere to go."*

"Had it really been ten years?" he thought to himself as he wound through another stretch of Kentucky road. In so many ways it seemed like an eternity ago, and yet the pain and the memories were still so fresh. He turned the volume knob and let himself sink into the music. He was listening to Darkness on the Edge of Town, his go to driving CD when the evening turned to darkness as it would tonight. The music crept out of the speakers and seeped into him while he drove, giving him focus, at least for the moment. He looked down at his wedding ring and almost smiled. Returning his eyes to the road, he pressed back into the seat and accelerated.

The miles peeled back beneath his car as he ventured southeast. He chewed the foil wrapping of his gum to stay alert and focused his eyes on the road. Driving through the south was easily one of his favorite pastimes. He had made his first road trip through Kentucky when he was 17, finally stopping in Jackson, Mississippi to stay with an Uncle. At certain points in the road, the Appalachia's almost seem to rise up to meet you on the horizon line, and in other stretches, they flank you on either side, rolling and tumbling endlessly down the highway.

He turned off the highway at his exit and followed the road that would lead him to his destination. It was a familiar road, and a feeling of steady accord washed over him as he cruised through it, nearly there.

The road lay in the valley, between two massive, rolling green hills. The kind you can only find in the south. On the right, the hill rolled up into a swarm of trees at the top, with a path cut through the center. On his left was Harlan County's only graveyard, and it was in Evarts. Thirty minutes away.

Malcolm Evans stepped out of his sky blue ninety-eight Oldsmobile onto the gravel at the foot of the hill. It had been far too long since he made his last pilgrimage to the gravesite. Clarence Evans, his grandfather, the man who raised him, was buried near the top of the hill. He gave a quick glance at the wilting roses in his backseat and started walking.

The air was cool that Sunday afternoon, carrying the smell of freshly cut grass and the familiar scent of a nearby storm. The valley had always been a strangely peaceful place. When his grandfather was put to rest, he felt none of the uneasiness he had in the funeral parlor or in the church. Something about how the wind swept down to the road and floated out gently up the hills on either side. Serenity had power over the elements in the valley, and everything seemed to move and breathe together. A strange place for a graveyard.

Maybe it had something to do with eternal rest, Malcolm thought as he reached his grandfather's row. He would never forget where he laid his surrogate father to rest. Third row from the top, 6th grave in. He was nearly 60 years old when Malcolm was born, and after his mother died, he took him in. There they were, a 71 year old man and an 11 year old orphan standing on the cusp. Coping with disaster. Malcolm sat down next to the headstone.

"Hey pop." He said quietly, resting his arm on his knee. "It's been a while, I know. Life's been moving fast. I got married. Not to the last girl, but the one I met right after. 4th of July, three years ago. Oh, you'd love her. She's tall, gorgeous brown hair. She can cook like you wouldn't believe. I got a baby boy, too. Yeah, last week. If you couldda seen my face when I found out I was gonna be a dad!" He laughed.

He was wearing his grandfather's old Bomber Jacket from World War II, coupled with a shirt and tie. Chinos and black leather shoes to bring it together. He saw a picture of him in the Army, on base in the States before deploying to France, where he took part in the D-Day attack on Normandy. It had inspired him to at least try and walk in his footsteps. By now he was an Aircrewman in the Navy. He made first class in 7 years, keeping his head down and crashing through his advancements. After doing one tour as a prison guard on an Individual Augmentee assignment in Afghanistan, he had returned to the states where he settled down, and met Wendy.

"I hope you're proud of me. I'm walkin it just like you. Serving my country, startin a family, everything a man's got to do. I think about you every day. God, I miss you sometimes. Most of the time I'm alright, but there are some days…" He trailed off. "One little thing, one simple little thing will remind me of you and set me off all over again. It's alright though; Wendy helped me through almost all my rough patches. If it gets too bad I just go out on the water and fish. That always works."

He remembered the first time Clarence took him fishing. There was a river about 45 minutes up the road from their house, and on Saturday mornings, Clarence would get in the truck and go fishing while Malcolm finished his chores in the yard. It gave them both well needed time alone, as well as a chance for them to get personal exercise in. Already in his early 70s, his grandfather stayed fit by continuing his weekly schedule. Waking up early to cook breakfast, chopping wood for the fireplace and taking a daily walk around the neighborhood. On the weekends, he would drive down to the river and row upstream, against the current to warm himself up before he settled in to fish.

One day when he was 14, Malcolm was asleep in his room when he felt a hand on his shoulder. "Hey, Bud. Wake up. You wanna ride to the river with me?"

Malcolm shot out of the bed and rushed for his clothes. Looking at his watch he saw it was 4:30am. The sun hadn't even come up yet. He borrowed his grandfathers flannel shirt and skullcap to keep warm in the chill of the early morning. Clarence turned down the radio, "Roll down your window." He smiled. Malcolm complied, rolling down the truck window and sticking his head out a little. "Hey!" He exclaimed. "I can smell it! I can smell the river. How close are we?"

Clarence chuckled to himself, "About two miles out. That's cool, huh?" Malcolm nodded his agreement happily. When they reached a clearing in the trees, Clarence turned off the road and guided the truck down a path, through the woods and onto a 10x15 foot patch of gravel near the river's edge. The sky was beginning to lose its darkness, a pale gray taking over at the horizon; the sun would rise in less than an hour.

Malcolm remembered the way the rough, worn down handle of the oar cut into his hands. It was springtime, and since there wasn't much yard work to be done, his hands had lost their calluses over the winter. He didn't catch a fish that day, or the next time, but he would never forget that first day that his grandfather took him out fishing. They talked and Clarence regaled him with death defying stories from World War two, and from his 26 years spent in the coal mines.

Those were better days. And with every day that came after it they faded further and further into the past. He was the toughest man he'd ever known. And the kindest. Malcolm wished he could one day measure up to be half the man Clarence Evans was. Now he was ten years gone and he was forced to go on without his guidance. He had done well for himself, but that shining example his grandfather set gave him a goal to chase down. A goal that always seemed to be two steps ahead of him.

"Wendy was good for me after I came back from the Sand Box. She helped me turn all my energy and restlessness towards certain things I could actually put my hands on. We bought a house; I got rid of my debts. Paid everything off. I mean, you know me. I don't have a drop of slow-down in my blood. Hell, I got it from you." He shifted for a moment, pawing at the grass between his knees.

"I told you we had that baby boy last week…I'm not sure what to do. I mean, I got all the lessons I need from you, but I don't know how you did it. I'm not sure if I'm strong enough on my own." He swallowed hard, looked up toward the darkening sky and continued.

"Wendy had a rough time. The baby was all tangled up, and she was bleedin real bad. The nurses took me out of the room and made me wait in some other room. They were in there for a long time. Too long. I could hear her voice carryin all the way down the hall. When it stopped, I swear I knew what happened, but I had to be sure. I didn't want to know, but I had to be sure. If that makes any sense. I busted down there, but they had set some guys outside the door, and they were tellin me to go back to my seat. '*Go back to your seat.*' What kinda shit is that? That's my wife in there. My only child too. Everything I love is behind that door and they told me to go back to my seat?" He took a deep breath and looked over at the headstone.

"I rushed through, but the curtain was closed, I couldn't see anything but the sheets at the end of the bed. They were soaked through with blood. Something in the bottom of my stomach fell out, something worse than anything I've ever felt. Deeper than worry, deeper than fear. I don't know what it was, but I don't think I'll ever feel it again. The doctor came out and told me that she didn't make it. I guess her blood didn't clot when she got to bleeding like that. It all happened so fast. After that, it was a massive hemorrhage and she was gone. Then he told me they were able to save the baby, but he had to be moved to the ICU as soon as possible."

Malcolm's throat started to dry and close up. He coughed and straightened himself up. Even though an earth-shattering whirlwind was crashing through him, he never showed. He stayed composed, kept it together. His grandfather's inner strength had passed on to him, and his poise in the face of disaster was proof of that.

When his mother died, he knew Clarence was in pain. A great deal of pain. Suffering the loss of a child was one of the things that happened to other people, it was never dwelled on, never thought of, until it happened. His grandfather withdrew into himself, but refused to be brought down by the world. His responsibility to Malcolm had kept him from sinking into the depths. He brought the boy out from under the cloud of trauma, and made him strong in spite of what he'd lost. They leaned on each other, one got the son he never had, the other got the father he never had. The bond couldn't be stronger, even through the grave his grandfather gave him solace and direction.

He looked across the valley toward the other hill, the sunset was nearly over and the pink and orange hues were beginning to disappear behind the trees, being overtaken by a bluish gray sky. Clouds were rolling in behind him and the wind from down below began to pick up. He remembered the funeral procession that brought him to the valley the first time all those years ago. He remembered walking behind the casket as they put it in the hearse behind the church. He was numb with loss, until they reached the valley. It all melted away. Things didn't all of a sudden make sense, but he was much more calm about his solitude. It was here he came to embrace it.

• • •

His nose had been right; a light rain came in over the top of the hill and showered the valley. Malcolm hunched his shoulders up against the rain and turned his face towards the headstone.

"I'm not sure about the boy, pop. He ain't doin too hot. You know, I always thought I'd be like you were. Out there in the backyard, too fast for my years, teaching my boy how to hit a curveball. But he's sick, pop. He's hurtin, and he needs me. I gotta get to him. I know that's what Wendy would want. I only got through losin Mom because of you. After last week, I don't know if I could stand losin anything more. I think I might re-up. Do another IA or GSA; maybe even take orders over there. The money's good, and it's tax-free, I know I'll be able to provide for him if I'm pulling in that kind of change. I was thinking about getting out this go-around, but now I'm not sure. I really wanna do right by the boy, make sure he's taken care of, you know?"

He stood up and relaxed his shoulders against the rain. "Now I gotta go, you take care. Put in a good word for me up there alright? Watch over me on the highway, I'm tearin right out of here."

He walked down the hill steadily and made his way to the car. Pulling his keys from the pocket of the bomber jacket, he turned around and took one last look at the headstone. His vision was blurred by the rain, but he could still make it out. Sitting there stoically, enduring all elements, all seasons, and still standing as though it had been set the day before. He got in the car and revved the engine, thoughts still swirling around in his mind. But the knot in his chest that had been there before was now gone. He was at peace on the inside. He knew he'd make the right choice. Danger never worried him, but uncertainty did, and now it was gone, swept away with the western wind. As he turned the radio up, he looked out the window at the graveyard and smiled. With the valley disappearing behind him, he pointed the car north and drove towards the hospital.

I Love You, Jim Morrison

"I'm the King of the Gutters, the Prince of the Dogs. One or the other, a ship in the fog..."

"Ahh, fuck me." He said, wind whipping him in the chest and face. He hunkered down to try and light his cigarette, to no avail. His head began to feel the rush of the coke, strangely conflicting with his drunken limbs. He walked the four blocks from the house where his band practiced, back to his apartment. He ducked into the alley and finally lit his cigarette.

The sun was shining deceptively bright that morning, and he had left without a jacket. In nothing but an open button up and some thin jeans, he had braved the weather. For the most part. He was too wasted to feel much at all. This had been a trend recently, and the reason the boys had kicked him out of the band. He had gone all Brian Jones on them and spun out of control into uselessness.

That was always the one rule, "When you can't handle your shit, then it's time to give it up or go." He went. Stumbling up the steps, he rummaged around with his keys until he found the right one and opened the door. He was suddenly bushwhacked with the smell of cigarettes, hash, and old rum. Flicking his cigarette into the flooded sink, he trudged across the floor and collapsed in front of an enormous poster of Jim Morrison. "Hey, Jim" he croaked. He sounded ashamed, as if talking to an old mentor. "It's me again. It's Nicky. I fucked up, Jim. I fucked up pretty bad this time. Too much blow, not enough music. What's the score? What's the balance? I mean, I feel like I'm hurting everyone around me, but I wanna have fun too, ya know?" He stared up at the picture, and the Lizard King stared back.

"Thing is, I'm alone. Sure there's a bunch of cool shit that comes with rock n roll, but there's the Demons too. I get lonely sometimes. I mean, Hell, **everybody** gets lonely, but I'm talking about some 'Only man in a crowded room' type stuff, man. But you gotta put on the macho bullshit, cause it seems like the whole world is watching. You gotta calculate. Ahh, you probably don't know what the Hell I'm talking about. You're Jim Morrison. Mr. Mojo Risin' himself. Rock God. Too cool for anything to faze you. I wish it was that easy for me." He stirred. "You want a drink? I'm a little fucked up, but I gotta level out. This blow is making me jittery. Teeth are starting to grind."

He wobbled to the kitchen, reaching for a bottle of rum and two glasses. Then he ambled through the fridge and produced two cans of sprite. Steadily a he could, he mixed the drinks, around half and half. Balancing himself, he half staggered, half swaggered back to the poster where he sat one drink down in front of Morrison and the other on the nearby coffee table.

"So yeah…" He started. "Loneliness. Let me tell you where it all started. It was wintertime, and it was colder than a witch's titty outside. Cold weather is always bad for lonely people, so I filled my nights with women wine and song, like any good musician would. It was the time of our first EP; it was the time of sex free of charge. (I'm not talking about money either), it was the time of the first 'Last' line, or drink, or injection. It was the time of the last kiss with the girl I loved."

. . .

"There was too much blow. I was snowblind to everything around me in those days. My girl had left me, and I had taken to the bottle pretty hard, and to the coke even harder. All that unrest fucked up my creative process, and I couldn't produce a new riff for five months. Five months! Luckily we were just trying to support the EP, and we took to the road. I found some great shrooms in Memphis, and, the women and weed were spectacular in LA. But it was all superficial. I just wanted to hold MY girl again…I won't say that there weren't times when I woke up feeling like I'd been nestled in the cleavage of Angels, but goddamnit did I miss her. The taste of her kiss, those dimples on her lower back. Iris. There couldn't be a more fitting name for a girl. The single most radiant, beautiful eyes I've ever seen. Before or since. She saved me from who I was going to be. That cheap old cliché of the wasted troubadour guitarist, trying to make his way home. Fuck that. I was an elegantly wasted guitarist in the peak of happiness, but I found a way to screw it up. My stupid mouth. My wayward heart. It all happened so fast. A flirtation here, a kiss there, next thing I know, I'm on top of some smacked out model with dark circles around her eyes for no other reason that she loved our show. Not my fault. **Christ,** I'm such a fuck up."

. . .

"I guess there just comes a time where if you're not careful, you become a cartoon; a gross exaggeration of yourself. Sometimes it feels like I'm doing this awful, gaudy impersonation of who I really am." He confessed. He knew for a fact that Morrison knew what that was like. Getting fat and drugged up, being crushed under the weight of his own image. Nicky took a deep drink from the rum, feeling better now that these things were off of his chest and out in the open. It was therapy, really. Guilt and shame were bogging him down, so he self-medicated to suppress those Demons, and the work suffered. In the weeks leading up to the guys kicking him out of the band, he'd been difficult, combative, and belligerent. Showing up late to practice, and arguing nonsense once he got there. He was paranoid. By now, the only person he can trust is a six-foot poster of Jim Morrison tacked up on the wall in his ratty apartment.

He poured another drink and felt himself leveling out. When he sat back down in front of the Lizard King, he avoided eye contact. He struggled with what he was about to say, but realized it would be cathartic and straightened up, taking a breath. "Iris kept me balanced. There was never too much pressure with her. When things got bad, they got worse, but when things went well... Damnit, you couldn't stop us. I never went too far over the line when I was with her. At least not til the end. I know I sound all pathetic and obsessed with the past. I can hear it too. But if you could just see her. Those eyes. That greenish-blue. God, she was beautiful."

Then he went quiet for a moment, thinking to himself. "I think, maybe, it's different for everybody. We've all got our centers, the things that keep us on the line for so long. That keeps us from falling off on either side. Once you lose it, though..." He trailed off. "Once you lose it, it's a hard way to fall. A long way down." His vulnerability had gotten the best of him, and he finally heard out loud what he'd been feeling and thinking for the last year.

He felt frustrated, exposed. Mad at the fact that it took him this long to come to terms with himself. Now that it was too late. He grabbed hold of the table and eased to his feet. Walking to the kitchen he realized that his anger and shame had left him feeling sobered and empty. He lit a cigarette. They always said admittance was the first step towards something big. He just didn't know what his something was. Finishing the rum, he doubled back to the living room to grab the bottle and the extra glass. Reaching down, he discovered that the glass of rum he'd poured for Morrison at the beginning of the night was empty. His hand drew back in shock. Looking around for a moment, he grabbed the glass and shook off any questions, "Must've drank it earlier…" he mumbled to himself.

He opened a cabinet above the fridge and grabbed a small orange bottle. He'd done enough already, and it was time for bed. Standing over the sink, he cupped a handful of cold water and swallowed the oxy's. "Well." He said to no one in particular, "Tomorrow's another day."

Sister Morphine

"He healeth the broken in heart, and bindeth up their wounds"

Malcolm Evans woke up in a haze, not recognizing where he was. He felt like he was sitting in the middle of a great fog; nothing around him was clear or tangible. Then it happened. Pain sprinted up his spine and crashed into his skull, jangling his brain around against its walls and blinding him. He tried to bring his hands up to cover his face, but only one arm responded. He felt the awkward jerk of a needle inside his other arm and quickly returned it to his side. Looking down, he saw the blood soaked bandage covering his left shoulder and running the length of his bicep. It was stained a dark crimson; it needed redressing.

Running his good hand across his chin he felt hair; stubble indicative of a week's growth. He'd been in and out for at least five days. The pain was dizzying in his head as he tried to think, and then he heard a voice come from the haze. A low, guttural moan from across the room. Malcolm squinted as best he could in the direction of the voice without setting off the crashing symphony inside his skull.

He was in a hospital bed at Landstuhl Regional Medical Center, Germany. Suddenly his surroundings began to make sense. He strained to remember what happened to place him on the sidelines.

There was an explosion in the prison where he was standing guard. They were mustering new detainees near the entrance area, sometime around 0900. He was walking away from the door when he heard shouting, and turned just as the bomb went off. Malcolm scoured his thoughts. The air itself had gotten hot. Not like the desert heat. This was unique; he'd never felt anything like it before, a searing, white hot wave went through the air as the sound of the bomb assaulted his eardrums.

The blast ripped through the air, kicking dust and shrapnel in every direction. The ripple effect lifted the table and everyone near it into the air before viciously slamming them back down like ragdolls. Malcolm tried to turn back around and dive for cover, but a wayward piece of shrapnel charged across the room and crashed into his arm. The blast itself is probably what shook his brain. That or the impact when he fell unconsciously to the dirt floor.

He leaned back in the bed, worried about the other men. How many had survived? Was he alone? His thoughts shifted for a moment to the dull throbbing pain in his left arm. He looked down and followed the needle's path, up the tube and directly to the morphine drip. The drugs weren't working.

He could feel the surgeon's work, where he was sown back up. He could feel the ghost of the medication working on the wound, since the pain wasn't so immediate. Instead there was the slow, dull, thump just beneath the skin. He grimaced and tried not to focus on the pain, but the pace of the throbbing in his arm was in rhythm with his pulse. Kicking like a giant bass drum, the beat overtook his entire upper body. His head swam and he laid back down.

The war was nearly over. Malcolm cursed to himself as he thought about what he could've done to avoid the explosion. He only seethed for a moment, settling down soon afterward to think about what would come next. His IA would be canceled, and he would return to his squadron in the States. If he could make a strong recovery, he would be fit to fly again upon his return. The risks of the job had become more of a concern now that he was a father. He knew what it meant to be orphaned, and he refused to put his son in that same position.

The boy was staying with the family of one of Malcolm's friends from the squadron. They had grown close during the last deployment and he had offered to keep the boy while Malcolm was in Afghanistan. Wendy's death had left him shaken, but he knew his responsibilities came first. He had to shoulder his grief and journey to the desert where he could best provide for his son. The eminent danger and hazardous duty pay, the tax free, and the eval and award points a second tour in Afghanistan would give him. It would give him more medals. It would help him advance.

He would be decorated, sure. But at what cost? He prayed his arm would make a full recovery, toying with the Saint Anthony around his neck. He wasn't getting any younger, and each wound, each bruise was taking its toll on his body. How much more could he take before he final broke and folded under the pressure? Uncertainty felt foreign to him, it was rare that he felt it, but in the vulnerability of his injury he could sense it sneaking up on him.

It was then he decided the payoff wasn't enough to compensate for the risk. He wanted to watch his boy grow up; he wanted to be there even longer than his grandfather was there for him. He had to get out. As he sat up in his bed, thousands of miles from home and thousands of miles from the front, he tried to clear his clouded mind and make a plan.

He would get out at the end of his contract. There weren't many jobs on the outside, but Malcolm had a unique set of skills that would allow him to pick up odd-jobs anywhere. He would be relying on sheer luck and tenacity to get him and his son through the rough times. There was enough grit in him to overcome his troubled past, so he knew there was more than enough now. This would be the test, to see if he still had it in him. The first thing he had to do was let his Chief know as soon as he came back to work. There was time enough on his contract for one last deployment, and that was it. He was finished.

As he grunted his approval of the plan, pain shot through his head again, clamping his eyes shut and baring his teeth. It was nearly unbearable; he used his good hand to hold his head as he tried to rock the pain from his body. Back and forth, side to side, and soon the pain subsided.

A nurse entered the room about ten minutes later to check on the moaning man across from him. She bent over him and did something Malcolm could not see, before adjusting his medication and to his surprise, gently, lovingly running her hand through his hair. There was pain in her eyes, a woman's empathy. That was the strongest emotion in the world. Malcolm took all of it in before calling out to her as he struggled to sit up.

"Excuse me, miss." He croaked. His voice hadn't been used in a week and his throat was as dry as the desert that wounded him.

She looked up and turned to his direction, seemingly surprised to see him awake.

"I don't mean to bother you, but it's my arm and my head. I'm in a world of hurt, and I'm just wondering if there's any way to up my dosage."

She smiled tenderly and walked over to him. Her hair was short, falling just above her earlobes. Malcolm saw there was something genuinely sweet about her. She was around 5'9, slim built, and American. She had a nice face. Not a beauty queen by any means, but a good face and a gentle jaw line. Malcolm liked looking at her.

"Of course, sir. I'll just adjust the drip on the machine here." Immediately he knew she was from the south. She had traveled quite a bit as a nurse, diluting her accent, but the slight twang in her voice betrayed her.

"And now…" She waited a moment while she fiddled with the machine. "You see this setting? Now you can adjust the drip yourself. But be careful, there is a maximum. This should curb your pain and take care of any problems you have. If you need me again, just use the buzzer."

She looked down at his chart. "You have a good day, Petty Officer Evans. Take care now."

He looked at her face again and croaked out another word.

"Tennessee?" he smirked

Her eyebrows rose. "Very good, Mr. Evans, very good."

He gave a smile of satisfaction and lay back in his bed, looking up at the ceiling.

He closed his eyes and felt the beating of his heart and his wound merge into one continuous ***thump.*** He knew that it would heal in time, and that when that time came, he would fly back home and prepare for the challenges that lay ahead. It would be yet another hard road, but that seemed to be all he ever traveled on. His plans were final and he knew in his soul that his last deployment would be the hardest, the most hellish, because of the void that awaited him on the other side of it.

• • •

As the morphine finally began to take hold, Malcolm relaxed and cleared his mind. His last thoughts before the darkness were dreams of his son in America.

A Quiet Place

"Well..." he said to himself, wincing along the rough shoulder of the highway. "Should've known it'd come down to this. Only old men get to die in their sleep."

It was too dark to see, but he was certain he was leaving a grisly trail as he bled down the highway; feeling weaker with every step. The charred and twisted remains of his car lay glowing about fifty yards in the distance, groaning and crackling in the dusk. The accident itself had been trivial. No time to place blame, only time enough now to get off that damned highway. Find a quiet place to die.

Every man knows the feeling when it comes, life leaving you like air rushing from a punctured tire. He'd never felt it before, but when it came he recognized it immediately. Taking every bit of concentration and strength, he put one foot in front of the other and strained to keep his eyes open against the blood and darkness.

"Chevron" he thought to himself as he caught sight of a filling station in the distance. He just needed to get to the empty lot next to the Chevron. Then he could rest...

His goal now in sight, he turned his mind to other things, trying not to count his steps.

"Ex-wife" No...

"My father" No...

"My first child" No...

This wouldn't do. His last train of thought could not be of leeches or the Dead. His mind raced for a solid memory.

Something to soothe him, to comfort him. He groped in the darkness for a piece of the past. Then it hit him. He concentrated on his grandfather's cabin home where he spent summers as a boy. Visits in the fall… Around this time of year. The weather had started to turn and the leaves were just beginning to fall. The vast backyard that led into the woods.

Soon he was back on the trail going deeper into the woods. His steps labored because the hand-me-down work boots were heavy on his skinny young ankles. He looked around and took it all in. The wind blowing softly, but just enough to rustle the leaves on the trees and the ground, carrying that autumn smell into his nose. After a stretch, he came to a fork in the trail.

"There's a lake about a mile east of here. Down that stretch of road." He remembered to himself. He decided to reminisce, and took the turn down the dirt path towards the river.

Many memories came back to him; too many to single out, as he took a feeling of weightlessness down the trail. The river's scent appeared a little further down and he was reminded of many early fishing and hunting lessons with the old man. He had his first kill here so many years ago.

He remembered it well. The buck had wandered into the very clearing that he was coming up on, bowing majestically to quench it's thirst. The old man put a heavy hand on his shoulder in the cool autumn morning. Wordlessly telling him to keep steady, breathe, and look through the target. He confirmed his grip on the Winchester, found the buck in his crosshairs, and took a deep breath….

The clearing lead his toes up to the river's edge, and he looked around. He could almost see the blood still glistening on the ground where the buck had fallen. He squinted at the ground and the leaves and dirt faded, leaving only a crimson stain visible in the flickering glow of nearby neon lights. It had been a long walk. His breath was short and his body had grown weary.

. . .

"I'm so tired…" he whispered.
     "It's time to go home."

The Fifth Round

"Everyone has a price...nothing is free. Not even me."

The arena was empty. Or it may as well have been. There was a distinct feel of emptiness in the arena that night. Malcolm Evans sat in his corner of the ring, blood and sweat mingling on the ridge of his brow. He chewed the end of his mouthpiece, trying to calm himself down. Boxing was a pastime of his when he was a teenager. His grandfather gave him his old gloves when he expressed interest. Times were different now; the success of mixed martial arts had firmly shoved boxing in a corner. Seats were empty, sales were low, and promoters were desperate. Malcolm was just trying to make some extra money to support his son.

It had only been six months since he'd been discharged, but things had gotten tough. The connections he once had begun to corrode and doors were closing in every direction. Places that were once hiring were now full, and back door jobs had gotten too hot back home. Boxing was one of the few things that could carry him through until an opportunity presented itself.

His love of the sport didn't translate into this particular match, or this particular arena. It had become a job, another obstacle to climb, another bump in the road. He opened his mouth and his trainer splashed lukewarm water down his throat.

The halfhearted ring of the worn out bell did nothing to rouse or motivate him. He knew what had to be done. The apeish Texan came lumbering out of his corner towards him, shoulders rolled forward, breathing heavy through his mouth. Malcolm danced under a right cross and away from a wild jab, tagging him in the ribs twice as he emerged on the other side of the ring. The crowd stared blankly on, most of them looking down at their cell phones, ignoring the match.

The Texan sprang to life and closed in on him near the ropes. He took up too much space to simply slide around, so Malcolm put his guard up. A massive glove came crashing into his forearm, and yet another came heaving towards his ribs. Lowering his elbow, Malcolm absorbed the blow. Before his gloved hand could make it back to his face, a wild, brutal punch landed just above his jaw. His vision blurred. His legs lost sensation, and the yells of the corner-men began to fade.

Silence.

"Damn it. Not yet." He told himself as his legs returned to life. He staggered across the ring, pursued by a bloodied pink ape with a southern accent and a fierce underbite. He managed a wild punch that dragged worn leather across the Texan's open eye, sending him reeling backwards, howling. Having bought himself some time, Malcolm tried to adjust his eyes after taking a heavy blow. He hunkered down, ready for the second assault, when the bell rang.

It was more of a wheeze at this point. The arena was dusty and old, only a few years from being closed down and everyone knew it. There would be no local movement to preserve the place as a piece of history, it would simply fall prey to the wrecking ball and be replaced by a liquor store. The stale smell of sweat lingered when there wasn't a fight, but that night, Malcolm smelled blood. He knew it was his own. It was a smell he'd grown all too familiar with in the last few years. He eyed the scar on his left arm.

He surveyed the gym and sighed at the pathetic crowd

that had been drawn. The low hats and cigars were ever-present. They didn't even count at this point. Spectators were lower than ever. Even the local paper had given up on actually going to the fights. He sat on his stool and let his hands drop on either side of his legs.

As the fifth round began, the referee gave him a quick look when he rose from his corner towards the center of the ring. There was a tension in the air, crackling like dry lightning. Cigar smoke drifted overhead. Everyone in and around the ring seemed to be clued in. The audience did not take note.

The Texan strolled up to the center of the ring, ready to polish off his opponent. His eyes grew wide when he saw the muscles in Malcolm's shoulder ripple underneath the skin. The deafening smack of leather on flesh echoed through ought the gym, grabbing everyone's attention for a brief moment. That was for Pride's sake. Blood splattered down on the mat. The Texan's knees wobbled, his eyes watered. A look of pure confusion washed over his face as he staggered around in place. Malcolm did not follow through with the knockout punch. Instead he waited for the heavyweight's onslaught. A crushing three-hit combo to the ribs, a right cross to the jaw, and then he grabbed a hold of him. Hugging him against the ropes. The big man was tired.

There was no finesse to his fighting style that Malcolm could observe. But he had power. He let his head rest on that massive, sweaty ham hock of a shoulder until the ref came to break it up. Sweat and blood mixed in a trail down his face that he squinted away. He made a silent prayer that his legs hold him up for a just a while longer. Just long enough to collect the check.

The pattern continued for a few minutes, until there were only two left in the fifth. The ref shot them each a look and barked for the fight to continue. Malcolm wearily approached the Texan, who was sweating and breathing hard, nearly doubled over from fatigue. A missed jab, a wild haymaker, and then he saw it. That goddamned right cross. He saw it coming from a mile away, and he thought of at least six different ways to dodge and counter. But Malcolm Evans held his ground.

When impact came, the glove hit him head on, taking up his eye, cheek, a part of his nose, and the top of his lip. Everything went red for a moment and then he felt his legs go weak. The Texan looked unsure for a moment and cocked a fist back for another blow before he looked in Malcolm's eyes. He leaned back and let his legs crumple helplessly beneath his weight, tumbling slowly towards the mat. His head bounced off of the surface and blood flew up off of his face, only to drop back down. The Texan gave a sigh of relief.

The ref started the count, a clear sound of relief in his voice. Noise was coming from each corner, his trainer was screaming for him to get up. The Texan's corner was rejoicing. The crowd seemed no different than it was ten minutes earlier. Malcolm stared up into the ceiling lights, noting how many bulbs had gone dead since the last fight. As the count reached ten, he closed his eyes and relaxed his breath, trying to let his mind stray for a moment. His thoughts were away from the gloating Texan, away from the gym, away from the fights, away from Afghanistan. He thought of the promoter in that dingy office across town, desperate for a profit. Was it the right thing? He thought of the $4,000 he could now use for his son. He thought of his $4,000 and tried to smile.

Invitation

The bar was nearly empty as he slid to the bottom of his eleventh drink. He looked at the now crinkled and abused plain envelope on the table before him and another pain dashed across his chest. He had already woken up in a foul mood that morning; a ghost of a hangover floating around his temples and bad memories lingering from years gone by. He had tried to ignore it. Treating the morning like any other, he spent nearly an hour at the piano, slowly rocking himself awake with slow blues and Ellington Jazz. This worked for a while, but there was a fleeting, almost casual feeling of dread that remained in the corners of his mind.

He had roused himself enough to get to his feet and check the mail. Walking across the hardwood towards the front door, he saw light playfully coil through the glass at the top of his door. He stepped outside and paused for a moment, letting the Nashville sun warm his face and then walked lazily across the yard to the mailbox. He opened it and sorted through the junk mail and the increasingly irregular postcards. Then there it was, staring up at him. This little white envelope. Raising an eyebrow, he opened it slowly and nearly dropped it when he read the card.

It was an invitation. His presence was cordially requested at a wedding. Or rather, *the* wedding. Here he was being formally asked to RSVP to the wedding of the only woman he'd ever loved.

Over the years he had been slightly successful in burying that pain and other heartaches. To drown them in rich bourbon and smoke; dirty blues and nameless women. But no amount of vice or distraction could stop the sudden swell of agony rising in his throat. As the name finally registered in his brain he realized that he'd seen the guy before. He'd seen them together at The Stage on a night he happened to be playing, and he'd wanted to tear his eyes out right there in the middle of his set. "*But then...*" He thought, clutching the envelope. "*Who's ever good enough?*" He tried to make her just another link to the past, but her memory refused to be anything but his biggest landmark; towering over every romance like some tragic monument to lost love.

Last call rang out like a shot in the dark, snapping him out of his daze. He closed his tab, and staggered out into the hot southern night like some drunken reject from an early Tom Waits song.

Once he'd made it back to the house he collapsed onto the bench and ran his hands across the top of the baby grand. This was it. That moment he'd dreaded for so long had finally come, and it was time to man up and make a decision. He had half a mind to rip up the invitation, drink a half bottle of whiskey and tear up the highway to Atlantic City and ride out the weekend trying to forget. But it didn't seem right; something told him he had to be around for it. Closure, or something like it.

He lit a cigarette, letting the smoke whirl and dance around his face and head in the dark room. He didn't know if he would be able to stomach the whole thing. The pomp and grandeur of it all, the dog and pony show before the dagger. "*Oh, God...*" he thought. What about when the preacher asks all the assholes, drunks, ex-boyfriends and college flings to embarrass themselves by professing their love in the Zero Hour? With no chance of redemption or pity? The idea was about as fun as a barbed wire hula hoop.

After five long years of uncertainty, he had to go. A

major chapter in his life was closing. Something inside was pulling him there, if only to finally bury the past. He stubbed out his cigarette in the ashtray atop the piano and went to his bedroom to drag out his old suit.

. . .

He slept terribly that night and couldn't get back to sleep when he shot awake at 7:30 in the morning. The wedding started around One O'clock at Woodmont Baptist Church. Sliding his feet out of bed, he shuffled to the bathroom and climbed in the shower. It had been too long since the last occasion that inspired him to clean up. It was either pure luck or discomfort that caused him to shave for a particular event, but this was different. It was time to step out like the old days, back when he had a reason.

He wrapped himself in a towel and stood in front of the mirror. His face didn't yet betray his age, but his eyes bore a weariness that told stories that crow's feet and smile lines never could. He shaved with the straight razor for the first time in months, running carefully along his face and chin. It was soothing, the precision and the care he had to take. A splash of aftershave would carry him through. He brushed his hair and went to his bedroom to put on the suit.

. . .

The old Brooks Brothers had never let him down. A good, well-cut jacket with thin lapels and subtle shoulders with pants that fell right at the top of his shoe. He buttoned his French-cuffed shirt in the mirror, and donned the jacket, pulling the excess cuff through the sleeve. Grabbing a black tie from the closet he executed a respectable half-Windsor and opened the drawer for his cufflinks.

Wearing the suit brought an old feeling back to him. Not quite confidence, but a shred of pride or self-respect began to return. It was only 8:45 after all that ceremonial dressing, so he decided to shine his shoes and play the piano before heading out the door.

The day was warm and beautiful. Spring was ending and giving way to summer and Nashville took on a bright and healthy look as the sun hung gracefully over the skyline. Dogs were barking as he got into his white-washed Cadillac CTS and started down the road. He was still feeling raw and wounded, and apprehension nearly took hold of him as he cruised through the streets. He decided he would wait and only sit through the end of the ceremony.

Stopping off to grab a bite to eat seemed to calm him temporarily. His hands had become tight on the steering wheel and were aching faintly. He had two beers with his meal and decided that it was time. Leaving a few dollars under the empty glass, he made his way back to the car.

Woodmont Baptist Church is a massive structure of graceful beauty, sitting grandly and proud just a few feet from the street. People were gathered outside with flowers, smiling and talking amongst themselves. He parked across the street and waited in his car for a moment, leaning back in the driver's seat and exhaling deeply.

Just as he had summoned his courage and got out of the car, the doors of the church burst open and a crowd seemed to erupt from the vestibule. They were led by the Happy Couple. They were descending the steps in a shower of rice, cheers and applause. He couldn't help but notice how happy she looked, her smile radiating across the street and stinging his chest. She was hand in hand with her Groom, who was grinning like a fox in a hen house.

When they reached the bottom of the steps there was a brief pause for hugs and congratulations before they got in the car and led the way to the reception. She seemed to sense something and looked up while her new husband continued hugging and shaking hands. For a suspended moment, their eyes met across the street. Her face held immediate recognition, but she decided instantly not to wave or gesture.

He was leaning against the driver's side door with his hands in his pockets, looking right back at her as lovingly as he ever had. His face held a barely-there smile, but his eyes seemed sad, pained. He gave a slight nod in recognition and congratulations, and she smiled as she turned back to her family.

No one had noticed the fleeting exchange, and the Happy Couple piled into their limousine and rode off to the reception with the rest of the party in tow. He watched as they drove away into the warm afternoon and the rest of their lives, and he realized it was time to begin the rest of his. He took one last look at the cars disappearing down the street and drove off in the other direction towards the highway.

Eggnog

*"And I am in the twilight of my youth,
not that I'm going to remember..."*

Snow was still falling outside as the party wound down. Charles Robinson sat at the head of the table, and was being prompted to make a toast. He stood shakily to his feet, clasping the bottle of rum in his hand, and looked around the room, exhaling deeply. "Well..." He started, scratching the back of his head, "I wish I could say that all of you here were valued friends. That each and every one of you have always been there for me, or were even worth a shit when the time called for you to be. But that would be a boldfaced lie. Most of you **aren't** worth a shit. You miserable bastards. You flakes. You fair-weather friends. You are gnats on the horse's ass that is the world, and I'm ashamed to know you."

Silence.

Then the group around the table burst into rowdy, drunken laughter and applause, and Charles put out his cigarette and walked out into the snow.

• • •

He had been great once. A freewheeling novelist and occasional journalist with a biting wit and a powerful pen, but there had been too many bridges burned, too many girlfriends stolen, too many drinks and doses over the edge. Too many fuck-ups. Now he was working at "Underground", a major mainstream magazine for people who still wanted to feel edgy and current in their pretentiousness. He hated damn near every person associated with that rag. They all knew who he was when he came on board, and a big deal was made, some of the staff members being "fans" of his made it extremely awkward for him the first week.

They were idiots. Pseudo-intellectual little shits from all across the country, rolling in their parent's money and "rebelling" against their parents' conformist ways. Half of these bastards were Vegan. The others were the type of people who make it a point, a *very strong* point, to tell you how much they "just don't care" about anything. The people who are way too in-your-face about being atheists. Smoking American Spirits, whining platitudes about the government and regurgitating opinions they heard on NPR. Bastards. Charles felt trapped; and he shrugged his way through the work, churning out mediocre pieces that were far below his talent.

He would haunt the bars, using the only two exciting vices he had left. He'd drink long into the night and then slide up next to a girl at the bar, and flip to auto-pilot as his default charm sunk in. This night it was an actress, or a cocktail waitress... She did more of the latter, but defined herself as the former, as most cocktail waitresses in the city do.

"I danced for a while, through middle school up into High School... Then," She smiled and took a deep breath, "I just got the bug!" Her hands fidgeted excitedly around her vodka cranberry, fingers wiping away the perspiration on the outside of the glass as she spun it slowly in the palm of her hand.

Charles eyed her up and down; she certainly had a dancer's body. Slim but strong, smooth, gorgeous legs and a toned midsection. Unlike the gymnast type, dancers usually avoid the curse of the flat chest. She was no exception, filling out her dress perfectly. As he thought about all the filthy, depraved things he wanted to do with her, her tidal-wave monologue about acting and her undying passion for it was crashing on the rocks of his defense. He wasn't even sort of paying attention. Not even a little bit. He made the obligatory "direct eye contact" about every 5 seconds, to keep the illusion of attentiveness going, but nothing she said even registered once in his brain.

He felt cold, detached. He was bored and kind of lonely, so he filled his nights with wicked, debaucherous, anonymous sex and a dizzying cocktail of drugs. By now he knew that every woman had some sort of kink or fantasy of some sort, and he obliged nearly every one of them. He had choked, spanked, bit, spit on, and hogtied his was through half of the city already. None of it mattered, though. Just something to pass the time. He wondered what her kink might be. As he pondered whether he would have to use the ping pong paddle or the baby-leash this go around, he heard the tell-tale heavy sigh just before a long-winded story wraps up. "… and that's pretty much what brought me to the city lights!" His eyes shot up to hers and focused, then smiling, he gently took her hand and caressed her fingers with his thumb. "I absolutely *love* a woman who is passionate about her work. Who's passionate about her *calling*." He corrected.

She swooned a bit, and tried to hide it, but he knew his window was open. "Look," he said, leaning back in his chair, "These drinks are getting a little pricey, and I've got a better bar at my apartment. Would you wanna-" "Yes." She answered before he could finish, then blushed at little at her eagerness.

The cab ride helped him intensify his flirtations; she laughed and slid closer to him until they reached his apartment complex. Charles tipped the driver generously and whisked the girl up the stairs and into his apartment. It was a very well put together and designed place, gray countertops and metallic silver refrigerator, microwave and stove. A fully stocked bar was in the living room area, with a flat-screen LED TV and a black leather couch. Ash trays outnumbered coasters on the glass table in front of the couch, and unlike most people's homes, Charles' apartment smelled like…*Nothing*.

They sat on the couch, drinking and talking while The Allman Brothers "Live at the Fillmore East" played in the background. He got up and walked towards the bar where he mixed her another vodka-cranberry. From a special drawer in the bar he pulled a small bag of blow, sprinkling some on the spotless counter. He cut a line using a fresh business card and used the metal straw from the drawer to heave it into his nose with a violent snort. A jolt went straight to his brain and his eyes immediately reddened. He offered her a line and started to make a Jack and Ginger ale for himself, but when he turned to look over his shoulder at her, he saw that she was standing right behind him. He sat the bottle of Jack back down on the bar and turned to face her. She gave a small smile and bit her lip as she drew closer to him, he could feel her breath on his neck. "Well…" he started; she quickly shut him up by pouncing and pressing a violent, meaningful kiss on him. He grabbed her, lips still locked, picked her up, and walked over to the couch where they crashed down onto the leather cushions.

. . .

The next morning he woke up when the sun stung his eyes through his bedroom window. They had made it to the bed, apparently, and the night started to come back to him. He turned and saw that she was still lying next to him, totally naked and sleeping soundly, brilliant red hand marks around her neck. His eyes widened in fear for a brief second before he put his ear to her lips and waited. After hearing regular, healthy breaths, he picked his head up and smiled devilishly to himself. "Chokers" he laughed quietly. Getting out of the bed, he popped two oxy's, stepped into a pair of underwear and walked down the hallway to the kitchen. His pants were on the floor, then his shirt, a thong, and then her dress. It was the dirtiest version of Hansel and Gretel he'd ever seen.

Moving into the living room, he sauntered over to the bar and downed his Jack and Ginger from the night before and grimaced; the soda had gone flat. He shook it off and walked into the kitchen looking for something to eat, when he saw the clock on the microwave. It was 10:00am. "Shit!" He whispered. He'd overslept and was now late for work. He looked at his reflection in the glass on the microwave, his eyes were bloodshot, but he didn't look horrible. Nothing a quick hairbrush and a pair of Ray Bans couldn't cure. He rushed back into his bedroom, slapped his Omega Speedmaster on his wrist, put on a light blue button up with a gray sport coat, slipped into his jeans and headed out the door.

As he took the elevator up to his floor at "Underground" he hoped he wouldn't run into anyone who'd ask questions, or speak entirely too loud. But sure enough, just as he turned the corner, Tiffany, the secretary, screeched an intolerable "Good Morning!" his way. His cover was blown. In a matter of seconds, the editor, *Anton* came striding up to him. "Charles… Good to see you this morning. You know it's, uhh 10:47. Umm, where have you been all morning buddy?" Charles **hated** it when he called him "Buddy". But he had to think of an excuse quickly. "I just started my next novel. Been up all night."

Anton's eyes widened, "Ch-Charles, that's great news! It's been what, 5 years since the last one!? Oh, man this is huge… I'm glad to hear it. What's it about?"

"I'll let you know when I know, ***buddy***."

"Ohh, one of *those*, huh? I know how it is. They just kinda take shape by themselves. Those are the best ones though. Well, I'll leave you alone, let the wheels keep turning. Keep me posted"

"Will do."

Anton walked away excitedly; he thought he had the first news of the first Charles Robinson novel in over 5 years. A big deal in the literary world. Charles had escaped again. He was notoriously private about his notes and manuscripts, so he wouldn't have to show proof of a damn thing. "*I might be able to milk this whole 'new novel' thing for a while*" he thought to himself.

It was all a sick joke. At least that's what he prayed for most of the time. The magazine was a self righteous, pseudo-trendy piece of filth that every hipster and assclown from SoCal to Soho read religiously. It was Rolling Stone for retards. And that's saying something. At least Rolling Stone *used* to be relevant. Charles took his bottle of Jack Daniels from the drawer and poured himself a drink. Taking a long pull from the chilled glass, he leaned back in his chair and waited for the day to end.

On his good days he felt indifferent to the state of his career and life, on the worst, he consistently tried to drown himself in an ocean of illegal drugs, alcohol, and horribly licentious, debauched sex with strangers. To some on the outside, it seemed like glory. Truth was, he was going through the motions of a former life. A life where he was motivated. Charles Robinson had simply run out of shit's to give. He was still sleepwalking through it, of course; appearances had to be kept. But anyone who knew him, or had the insight to look into his eyes, they knew he wasn't at the wheel anymore. He was buried somewhere deep beneath himself, hiding from the world.

He looked down into the glass where the ice was melting; it'd been an interesting day. Somehow skating by without writing a single word, on the merit of an imaginary novel. He had been great once, in total control. But those words rattled around in his head, beating him up, cutting him down.

"You're Charles Robinson, aren't you? Goddamn, son. 28 years old, and already washed up. It's been five years since that so-called 'Trilogy' of yours. When are you gonna write something that *isn't* in some slack jawed nonsense of a magazine? Every time I pick up an issue of Underground where you have the lead story, I have hope. And it's dashed every. Single. Issue. You're just pissing in the wind now. Get your shit together and **write** something, you goddamned loser."

A loser. He was a called a loser by Jacob Cahill. The Town Drunk. The fact that he was the town drunk in one of the biggest cities in America made it an even more crushing blow. But the bastard was right. Five years earlier, he'd written three books that totally changed the face of literature as it was known at the time. Garnering hundreds of thousands of fans, and hordes of imitators worldwide. He had sold the rights for one of the books to be filmed, pocketing a percentage of the gross. As it turned out, the film did decent at the box office, but became a cult phenomenon on home video, spawning douchey T-shirts and Facebook Statuses around the globe.

He looked down into the glass where the ice was melting; it'd been an interesting day. Suddenly, he was prodded in the shoulder by a slender, red-nailed finger. "Right?" a voice prompted him. "Huh? Yeah. Sure." He said, looking up. He was in a totally different place, back at his usual haunt, talking to some woman who appeared to be in her mid-thirties, dark brown hair, hazel eyes, wearing a sweaterdress that was hugging her in all the right places. "*Who the hell…*" he thought to himself. He was *just* in his office, having a drink, watching the first of the snowfall…

"You didn't hear a word I just said, did you?" She said, slyly. There was a pause. "No. No, I can't say I did. I zoned out there for a second. Occupational hazard. We tend to do that when we get an idea."

She eyed him, her bullshit radar blinking furiously, to the point of combustion.

"Yeah?"

"Yeah."

"What's your idea?" She said coolly.

Charles paused for a moment. "Man ogles woman's ladyparts in a sweaterdress and ponders how *anyone* can argue against Intelligent Design…"

She smiled, trying not to laugh too hard and encourage him. "*Smooth.* That just now come to you?"

"Been toying with it for a while. A good minute thirty, thirty-five maybe."

. . .

She'd been disarmed, despite her best efforts to stave off his charm. He seemed distant for most of the conversation; but when he focused his eyes on her, she saw him spring back to life, intensity rushing back into his face. But it was fleeting. She knew that soon, it would all fade away, and he would be the pleasing, one-size-fits-all man that she'd spotted across the bar.

She decided to take a chance anyway, and as the night wore on, she surrendered to his request to leave with him, on one condition, that they go to her house, instead of his apartment. He agreed, and as he picked up the bill, she went for a cab.

"*What the fuck am I doing*" He thought to himself as he adjusted himself to the backseat of the cab. He was safe in his apartment; he knew where all the traps were. This was something stupid he did in his younger days, couch surfing from town to town on tours. Forgoing the price of a hotel room and a stale, mass produced lobby breakfast for an awkward morning and a funny story when he got home.

She put her hand on his thigh and squeezed a bit, working her way up his leg until she found what she was looking for, and throttled it violently. Charles gave a muffled yelp and swallowed hard. He could only imagine what was in store for him in a few minutes. She teased and prodded him the rest of the ride, impatiently waiting their destination. When cab stopped outside her house, he tossed money at the driver and insisted that he keep the change.

They had barely gotten to the porch when he decided to try and gain the upper hand. Preempting her attack, he grabbed her and planted a firm kiss on her lips, working his way down to her neck, where he planted a small bite after each kiss. She let out a staggered exhale and wrapped her legs around his waist, and he slammed her back into the door, digging into her neck. She brought his face back up to hers and bit his lip ferociously, pulling her head back with it still between her teeth. When she let go, she dropped back down to her feet and opened the front door. They both entered, panting, drunken energy burning off and starting to tax their bodies. She led him through the house and into the living room where the couch was, and a stash of extra liquor. She shed the sweaterdress, revealing a devastatingly curvaceous, Mediterranean body. Charles noticed a scar, but didn't think anything of it, considering the circumstances.

She tossed her bra at him and waited. He tossed her back onto the couch and hovered above her for a second and then dove in to work. He peeled her underwear down with his teeth; a devilish pair of boyshorts, revealing a gorgeously shaped backside when something caught his eye.

. . .

"Is that a fucking playpen?!" he spat, ripping the panties from his teeth. She looked up. "You have a fucking kid!?" "I told you that!" She whispered lethally. "I *clearly* wasn't listening!" "Well keep your voice down, he's sleeping." She said. Not letting the interruption kill her mood, she reached out and grabbed her prey, pulling Charles behind it. He placed her leg on his shoulder and gave a thrust. She let out a moan louder than anything he'd just screamed earlier. His eyes got wide and decided he had to slap his hand over her mouth and press every time he drove into her. This went on for a solid half hour until she finally convulsed and collapsed into a violent sex coma.

. . .

He woke up in his apartment that morning with no recollection how he got there and a monstrous, hairy beast of a hangover. He shuffled around the place in his dress shirt and underwear, sunglasses glued to his face. As he attempted to eat his breakfast, he felt his whole body reel with nausea. Dropping the fork into his peppered eggs over-medium, he reached out for his glass. His head rocked and his eyes were dried out. He felt like his eyes were going to fall out of his skull, roll under his Ray Bans, and plop right into his tequila sunrise.

Light snow was falling, and there was more to come; only two weeks until Christmas.

. . .

When Monday morning finally rolled around, he realized he had to make the godawful trip back into reality and go to work. He shambled around the apartment, lighting a cigarette and walking to his closet. Holding it steady in his lips, he pulled down a black Valentino blazer and an "Exile On Main St." t-shirt and laid them across his bed.

Making his way to the kitchen, he opened his metallic gray fridge, grabbed four eggs, a pepper shaker, and a stalk of green onion. Everything was in its place, clean to the point of emptiness. The irony of the organization was not lost on a man whose life continued to slip into the absurd. Chaining another cigarette, he placed his pack of Red 100s on the counter and began to scramble his eggs.

After breakfast, he finished his Tequila Sunrise pitcher and placed it in the sink. He was running on schedule for once and decided to make a call to Viki, his go-to cab driver. As he stepped into his jeans, he told her he'd be ready for pickup in ten minutes if she could make it in 15. Easing the jacket over his t-shirt, he donned his Ray Bans and prepared for another day of empty, fruitless nonsense at a magazine he was beginning to truly despise, rather than pity.

The horn honked as soon as he stepped into the lobby and in a seamless stride he was out the door and in the cab.

"Mornin" Viki said, in a strained, rasped voice. "Sorry if I'm a little slow on the draw today, I picked up extra hours after the night shift."

"Don't worry about it" Charles muttered from the backseat. "You know where to go."

Charles liked Viki. She was a survivor. After spending six years in prison on a drug trafficking rap, she'd worked odd jobs until she found her fit in the taxi business. Addiction, abusive husbands, and health issues be damned; she was going to make her living no matter what.

"So how've you been, honey?" she said, taking the focus from her fatigue to his personal life.

"Coasting along. You know. The days are just kind of floating by. Nothing major."

"No new ladies in your life?" She teased, "It's getting real close to Christmas; if you end up all by your lonesome, you know who to call."

He gave a half smile behind his glasses. "Wouldn't be the first time, Viki."

He lit a cigarette and let his head rest back on the seat. It was getting colder every day. He didn't mind the cold, and rarely ever dressed for it, it was just the holiday season he didn't care for. When he exhaled a pillar of smoke, Viki made eye contact through the rear-view mirror.

"You wouldn't mind if I bummed a cigarette from you, wouldja honey?"

Charles didn't even answer her, reaching a cigarette over her right shoulder and into her hand.

"Thanks so much, sweetie."

"Don't worry about it."

Viki was nurturing by nature; after all of her kids left the nest, she started taking in children unofficially. Kids with no real direction who'd get in her cab, she'd take them under her wing and keep them out of trouble as best she could. Charles had the feeling that her biological children were probably embarrassed by her. Her profession, her record, the works. He couldn't see why. He *liked* her because of her ability to survive all that she had. Living with the cards she was dealt.

She'd been mothering him since he moved into the city. Although their friendship was one of profession, (Driver-Passenger) there was an intimate and unspoken understanding.

"There ya go. Back to the salt mine." She said as she parked outside the office.

He handed her the fare and stepped out of the cab. "Thanks, Vik. I'll give you a call when I'm ready to leave." He stepped up onto the curb and walked through the glass double doors. Putting his cigarette out in a potted plant in the lobby, he slid into the elevator just as it was closing.

Walking to his desk, he dodged "Good mornings" and mundane, obligatory questions about the weekend. He sat at his desk and stared at his computer screen. A black and white image of Keith Richards and Mick Jagger playing during the 1972 American tour. Maybe today he would change it back to the painting of Joe Strummer.

As he pondered what picture to put on his desktop next, Bobby, one of the youngest employees at "Underground" came bouncing up to him in a tight, light blue cardigan, eyes bright and breath short. "Charles! Charles. Hey. The Black Keys are doing a secret show in the city sometime in the next week, we just got the leak. I was wondering if you wanted the story, cause if not, I was gonna take it. I mean, I know you like that band and everything…"

Charles looked up with disinterest plastered all over his face. He'd barely been listening.

"Well?" Bobby asked. "Black Keys. Secret show. This week. Want the story?"

Charles took off his wayfarers and blinked. "Sure. Why not?"

"Awesome, bro. I'll let Anton know right away."

"Bro?"

"I was saying it ironically. I mean, I don't actually talk like that. I hate that whole frat scene…Backwards hats and Natti Ice."

"Shut the fuck up, Bobby."

. . .

Later that day he stepped out for lunch, which meant going for a few drinks at the pub around the corner. He despised most bar music, but this particular place had its own personal soundtrack of traditional Irish music, with a few Irish rock bands thrown in the mix. A bit of Pouges and Thin Lizzy, some Flogging Molly, even some Dropkick Murphy's for a little extra punch.

. . .

He fired down his fifth Jack and Ginger ale and looked around the bar. Checking his pockets for a lighter, he rummaged around for a second and produced a plain black Bic. It twirled between his fingers and came to rest in his palm. He sat it on the bar, staring down at it, ignited the flame and ran his fingertips over it before heading outside to smoke. The sweet lingering smell of cigarette smoke mixed with the city air, car exhaust, street vendors, sweaty tourists, and homeless people. A thousand different perfumes and colognes smashing into each other and creating a sweetly foul, yet distinctively familiar smell that hung in the air.

He went back inside, paid his tab and walked back around to corner to his office. As he walked up to the glass doors, he saw a tall, slender biracial girl standing in the lobby looking lost. He could only see her from behind, but something about her intrigued him. He was making his way to the elevator, after stealing a look at her from behind his glasses. She spotted him just as he was pressing the button to go up.

"Charles Robinson?" She asked, walking quickly up to him. Turning on his heels, the first thing he locked onto was her eyes. They were dark and intense, Charles wasn't sure if he was going to be kissed or stabbed. She stopped about a foot in front of him. She was ruthlessly good-looking; her jet-black hair hung to the middle of her neck, bright, incredible skin, and a mouth that was, in a word- *inviting*.

"Guilty." He said, eyeing her up and down. He thought of the cold, empty gray bed sheets in his apartment.

"I need to talk to you."

Charles raised an eyebrow in suspicion, but extended his arm anyway, ushering her into the elevator.

"You don't remember me at all, do you?" She asked as she walked in. Her voice was low and husky, captivating him even more.

"Honestly…I can't say I do. Though I'm sure it'll come back to me soon enough." He said, leaning against the elevator wall.

"Anita Jackson. Detroit. Two months ago. You were a guest speaker on another author's book tour. You told me to meet you at the after-party."

A slow sinking feeling started in his gut. "And then?"

"Wow. You are an asshole. We slept together."

"You're welcome?"

She stared daggers into him.

"I mean, I figured as much. What's the issue?"

"I'm pregnant."

"You're what now?"

"Pregnant."

"With a baby?"

"No. With a fucking moose. Of course with a baby, you retard!"

The elevator doors opened. Charles staggered out, his midday buzz ripped from his body.

"I think you've got the wrong guy, sister."

"Nope."

"Are you **sure** I'd be the father?

73

"What are you implying?"

"Nothing. Just that it could be a multitude of other-"

"I will kill you where you stand."

"***Shit***" He thought to himself.

He walked briskly to his desk with her closely in tow. Millions of questions and thoughts buzzed through his mind, but one came to the forefront. "How did you get here?"

"I took a bus." She said, matter-of-factly.

"You took a *bus*?" He said, in visible awe.

She opened her eyes wide and nodded sarcastically.

"Ok. Wait here. I've got to take care of something." He said gesturing to his chair.

He contemplated crashing out the window and making an escape, but they were entirely too high up for that. He found Bobby about to walk around a corner and grabbed his arm, swinging the boy around to face him. Bobby's eyes met his and he looked hurt, as if he either just finished, or was just about to cry.

"Oh come on, Bobby. Toughen up. Every time I see you, I feel like you're going to collapse into a puddle of tears and menstrual blood. It's embarrassing."

"Sorry, Charles."

"Don't be sorry. Look. You want that Black Keys story?"

His eyes brightened.

"It's yours. I just need a favor."

"What is it?" Bobby asked eagerly.

"There is a girl at my desk. Watch her til I get back. Don't let her out of your sight."

"Got it, Charles."

Charles gave him a nod and then dashed off down the hall in search of Anton's office. He'd been there once when he started working at Underground, but had avoided it at all costs ever since.

He passed the doorway and saw Anton hunched over his desk, listening to new music on his laptop with a look of pure disdain on his face.

"Anton. Hey!"

He didn't look up. He couldn't hear anything over the music in his earbuds.

"Hey!" Charles tried again. Realizing he was being drowned out, he called again. "You miserable jackass. You poorly endowed lump of human filth. You disgust me in every way pos-"

"Oh, Charles!" Anton said, looking up. He took the buds from his ears. "What's up?"

"I'm taking off for the day. Got a big breakthrough in the novel. I won't give anything away. But I will say this... Mother issues and a scrutinizing look at the perception of post-modern masculinity."

Anton nearly leapt from his seat. What are you standing around here for? Get going!"

Charles gave a hurried wave and rushed out the door, dialing Viki's number on his cell.

"Vik, I need you to come get me. I have someone with me, and it's very important that you *don't* ask questions."

He made his way back to his desk where Bobby sat awkwardly in front of Anita, avoiding her eyes. "Alright. Time to go. Come on." He said hurriedly, taking her by the arm, "Thanks, Bob" he said insincerely, and the two got back in the elevator.

"So what is this about exactly? An extortion deal with child support? Are you expecting a marriage proposal, what?" Charles asked, his heart finally climbing down from his throat.

Anita looked at him with inquisitive disgust. "What?

No. Jesus, you're an idiot. I came here because I thought you should know; and I need help… I want to get this taken care of."

Taken by surprise, he regrouped quickly. "So…What do you need? How much?"

"Well, the biggest part of my spending money went towards that ticket… I'm not sure if I'm even going back there."

"So you're thinking about staying in the city when all this is over?"

"Yeah, probably." She sighed. Her demeanor changed. Shoulders rounding and voice softening, she continued, "There's not much back there for me. I think I might start over here."

When she spoke, there was weariness in her eyes; age and experience beyond her years that seemed to reach out to him. A kindred spirit, lost in the wilderness of self-imposed exile.

They walked through the lobby and into Viki's cab. She sat idling outside, smoking and toying with the radio, settling on a soul station playing Sam Cooke. She looked back at them occasionally through the rearview mirror, trying to catch Charles' eye; looking for some sort of hint towards what was going on. He avoided her eyes, gazing out the window the entire time. The three of them drove to Charles' apartment in silence, except for the voices of Sam Cooke, Otis Redding, and Wilson Pickett.

• • •

"Nice place." Anita said as she came through the door, catching a view of the kitchen on her right and the television and couches straight ahead.

"Thanks." Charles said, taking off his sunglasses and heading for the bar.

"You don't entertain much, do you?"

"What do you mean? I have people over. At least twice a week!" He said, setting a bottle of Jack Daniels on the bar and reaching for a can of Ginger Ale.

"Ohh, I see." She said mockingly. "This has to be the emptiest, coldest apartment I've ever been in. Seriously, did you pick your furniture out from the picture of the apartment, or did you have Johnny-5 decorate?"

Charles was staggered for a second, retorting, "While I appreciate the 'Short Circuit' reference, and really, I do... Fuck off. My place, my style."

"If you wanna call it that."

"Do you want a drink or a punch in the gut?"

"I don't think I can take either, considering my 'condition'. Unless of course you just want to fling me down the steps and be done with it."

"I take the elevator, sister. I don't even know where the stairs are in this place."

She laughed a little and sat down on the couch. He took his drink and sat adjacent to her on the other couch, offering her a glass of Ginger Ale. She took it. They looked at each other for a moment, before Charles grabbed a remote and pressed play, starting Excitable Boy, by Warren Zevon. "Nice." She said softly, hearing the intro to "Johnny Strikes up the Band".

"Yeah. I've been in a '78 kind of mood today. I listened to 'Some Girls' when I woke up this morning. I might put on 'Blue Valentine' by Tom Waits later. You know-"

"We've got to talk about this, Charles." She interrupted. "I need money for this thing. And maybe, you know... if you can help... I need to get started on my own."

"Alright. I get it. I understand what we have to do. Why don't you stay here for a bit, until you find a place at least."

"Really? You'd do that?"

"Sure. What the Hell do I have going on?"

She laughed and shrugged her shoulders.

"Just wondering, but how much are we looking at here?" He asked.

"All in all? Around $5,000."

"Fuck."

"Yup."

. . .

She settled in that night. All she had was a small bag with a change of clothes and a toothbrush. Charles got decidedly and intensely drunk that night, abandoning the ginger ale mixer for ice and nearly finishing the fifth of whiskey, and fell asleep on the couch listening to Tom Waits. Anita woke up to go to the bathroom and found him slouched back on the couch, empty glass in hand. She gently took the glass from his hand and put it on a coaster on the table. Easing his body down so his head rested on the arm of the couch, she stepped back when he unconsciously put his legs up as well. She put a blanket over him and took a step back to look at him. Smiling to herself, she left him there to sleep it off.

At breakfast, he made his usual peppered eggs over medium, coupled with his hangover-busting pitcher of tequila sunrise. That morning however, he made bacon and toast to go with it, even sparing some of his orange juice for her.

"Do you always wear your sunglasses at breakfast?" Anita asked snidely

"Only when the sun's out." Charles affirmed flatly, raising his glass to her. He took a bite of egg and got up to go to the kitchen. Grabbing an orange bottle from the cabinet, he swallowed three pills quickly and chased them down with tequila.

"What's that?"

"Medicine." Charles answered coyly. "Doctor's orders."

She gave him a contemptuous look, scrunching her face up at him.

"It's oxycodine"

"Jesus."

"Hey, I'm a firm believer in the ol saying. 'Your body is a temple' and all that. My body, however... Happens to double as a laboratory. Constant, incessant experimentation." He said, taking off his Ray Bans and shooting down the rest of his tequila. He walked back over to her and grabbed the pitcher for a refill.

"So this is what you do all day, instead of writing books that are gonna change the world. You lock yourself in your ivory tower and get wrecked. Perfect."

"What else is there to do, hiuh? You expect me to be the pied piper to this pseudo-intellectual, shallow, self-absorbed, outspoken, *facebook* generation? I'm through being who everyone else wants me to be. I disappeared, dropped off the radar. They can't touch me now."

"So brave of you." She said, her voice dripping with sarcasm. "I can't say I don't respect you sticking to your guns. That's a courageous thing to do; but I will say that's the only courageous thing about you. It's okay though. You make an amazing breakfast."

They looked at each other for a moment; they were still sparring. Trying to figure out who was to be dominant in that monstrosity of a "relationship" they had.

The day wore on and Charles sat on the couch listening to music most of the day, drinking slowly and scribbling down notes at certain points during the songs. After changing out

James Brown: Live at the Apollo '63 and putting in Muddy Waters' "Hard Again" he half danced back to his seat, barely able to contain his excitement. Anita walked into the room and spotted him writhing around on the couch, glass raised, mouthing all of Muddy's lyrics to "Mannish Boy". She stood there laughing to herself for about a minute before he turned around.

"Oh, hey. Hey, c'mere, you've got to hear this record!" He said, eyes beaming. He gestured her over to him with his glass of Scotch. "One of my all-time favorites. Johnny Winter gets a legend back in the studio and just breathes life back into his career."

She smiled at him with wonder, she had never seen him this joyous or child-like before; but now she was noticing that whenever he talked about the music he loved, he lit up like Time Square at midnight.

He got up from his seat, setting his glass down on a coaster and walked over to her, grabbing her hands. "You've got to come *inside* the sound. Let the system do its job. Listen." Walking backwards, he pulled her into the circle of sound he'd created with his speakers. The bass rolled and punched, the harmonica slashed between left and right, and the vocals surged from the center, thumping and swaggering throughout the apartment.

As the last strains of "Little Girl" faded out, she looked over at him and leaned on his shoulder with hers. "You really love this stuff, don't you?"

"It's the only joy I got left in this world." He said with a smirk, taking a deep pull from yet another glass of Glenlivet. "Hey…" He started, "Have you ever seen 'The Last Waltz'?"

· · ·

Two weeks had passed and Anita had picked out a small house outside the city to start over in. Charles had Viki drop her off at the clinic to have her procedure and rode with her when she picked her up. Viki didn't charge for either trip. In those two weeks, Charles had eased off of the blow and the pills at Anita's request so he could survive to another Christmas. Anita went quiet for two days after they returned from the clinic. On the third day, Charles walked in on her packing up her things.

"Movin' out, huh?" He said, leaning against the frame of the door.

"Yeah." She said over her shoulder. "I'm gonna move in to that place in the suburbs."

"What, the city life's too busy for you?" He said with a minor smile. She didn't return the gesture.

"My cab will be here in a half hour." She said, zipping up the bag. She carried it to the door and set it down.

Charles lit a cigarette and poured himself a drink. A simple, strong and deep glass of scotch. Dropping an ice cube into the glass, he offered to make her one. "Since you're allowed now."

She nodded, and he mixed her a gin and tonic, setting it on the bar for her to walk over and grab herself. She came over to him and they sat down for a quiet last drink together.

The silence was soon broken by the sound of her phone buzzing against the countertop in the kitchen. Her cab was outside.

"Well," she said, standing up, "this is it."

"Yeah." He said, still seated. "Wait a minute; I want you to have something." He got up and went over to his massive CD and record collection. He pulled out a small 45" record. A single.

"Here" He said, handing her the record. It was "Roll over Beethoven" an original Chuck Berry single.

"Charles." She breathed. "This-this is one of your favorites. You said it's a classic."

"I want you to have it. You came at the right moment, Jackson. I'm seeing a little clearer thanks to you. Plus, if the money runs out, throw this sucker on Amazon and watch the cash roll in."

She tucked the record in her purse, walked to the door and picked up her purse. He followed her to the doorway and held it open for her. She slid up close to him and placed a quick, gentle kiss on his lips. When she pulled back, she slipped a piece of paper into his blazer pocket. "Don't be afraid to come over if you're alone on Christmas. I wouldn't wish this apartment on anybody. Especially at Christmastime."

He smiled and watched her walk down the hall. "Goodbye, Charles Robinson." She called over her shoulder. He just gave a slight wave and walked back into his apartment. From the window he watched the wind pick up and the snowfall get heavier; two days until Christmas.

• • •

He had spent Christmas Eve getting drunk on eggnog and watching the first two Die Hard movies. Later that night he braved the snow and went out to the bars, which not surprisingly, were empty. Everyone was with their families, or their lovers or their friends. But on Christmas Eve, Charles Robinson was piss drunk and wandering the streets of a frozen, deserted metropolis. With only $35 left in his wallet, he called Viki and pulled the piece of paper from the pocket of his peacoat.

8004 Sapphire street Northeast

Viki picked him up in the wee hours of Christmas morning; it was around 2am when he spilled into the backseat of her cab. He handed her the scrap paper and a cigarette. "Thank you, sweetie." She said in that warmly familiar, craggy voice he'd grown accustomed to. She drove him out of the city and across some country road before they came up to the street on the paper. Charles had called Anita's number early in the ride, but it was off. Straight to voicemail.

"Here you go, hun. 8004." Viki said, stopping in front of the house.

Charles handed Viki a twenty-dollar bill and staggered to his feet outside. The wind whipped his face and ears, so he turned up the collar on his coat and walked up the snowy driveway, lined by Christmas lights. He looked in the yard and saw the decorations; reindeer, elves, and multiples Santa's but thought nothing of it.

He rang the doorbell and then knocked, fidgeting drunkenly in the cold. There was shuffling behind the door, and then a light clicked on. The door opened and a middle aged man in glasses answered in his bathrobe, clutching a baseball bat. "Wh-What do you want?" he asked shakily.

Charles paused for a moment, bewildered by the appearance of the man in the doorway. "I'm... I'm looking for Anita Jackson."

"There's nobody by that name here." The man said sharply, panic rising in his voice. "We've lived here for five years. What are you doing here?"

There was a slow sinking feeling in the pit of Charles' stomach. "I don't know."

"Please..." the man said earnestly. "It's Christmas."

Charles turned around and sauntered down the walkway, turning out of the driveway and walking down the street into the snow. She got him. An expert move if there ever was one, a true hustle. The perfect con to match his hazy lifestyle. She had taken him for $5,000 and an original Chuck Berry 45". He doubted that she was ever even pregnant. Little by little, more doubt seeped into his mind. He lit a cigarette. All the changes he made because of this mystery woman appearing in his life. This supposed sign from above to curb his wicked ways and sober up, this godsend that would allow him to maybe write again someday. Someday when he was free of the booze, free of the pills, free of the powders. It was an impossibly iniquitous end to a seemingly serene salvation. He trudged through the snow down the center of the road; the plows wouldn't come for another three hours.

"*How could I have been so stupid?*" he thought. "*So willing to believe that life just works itself out. 'If you're having problems, just wait; someone will come along with all the answers and all the guidance you'll ever need. You may not even know it at the time, but their secrets will reveal themselves to you.'*" He was sickened by it. There were no cars on the road for as far as he could see, and the hill head of him was steep, he had a long walk to the nearest gas station. Hurling his cigarette into the snow and putting it out, he adjusted his collar again. "*Jesus.*" He said to himself, "*Merry Christmas, Charlie.*"

Bourbon Street

There was steam rising from the cracks in the New Orleans road when he woke up that morning. A thick and sweltering heat enveloped him as he groggily opened his eyes. The room was unfamiliar. Gaudy velvet curtains on the windows and wrinkled satin sheets on the bed confused him further. Looking up, he saw a mirror attached to the ceiling above the bed. He stared up at himself with a look of drunken bewilderment, seeing only a disheveled mess. His sport coat lay slumped behind his head, his shirt hung halfway off of his shoulder, with only a pair of underwear and one sock to clothe the rest of him.

He peered around in the darkness. There was sun trying to come through the curtains, but the room stayed in a sketchy dim light. Dual nightstands. One on either side of the Queen Size bed. A feeling of odd familiarity started to climb up his spine as he recognized the style of the room. The sense of hollow domesticity, like a dead-eyed motel. ...

Lying sprawled out on the tile floor he began to put it together. He had regained consciousness in a whorehouse somewhere in New Orleans.

This was not a normal hangover; his slowly palpitating heartbeats left evidence of an amphetamine comedown. That weird rhythm trying to synch itself back to normal inside his chest. He scanned the room for a cigarette and spotted a pack of Camel lights on the dresser.

He inhaled deeply, trying to collect himself. *"How did I get here?"* he thought. He attempted to retrace his steps through a depraved and hazy night tearing through Bourbon Street. His eyes were closed and he held his head with his smoking hand, leaning against the dresser.

His rumination was cut short by the clicking sound of high-heeled footsteps outside in the hall, and the door opened. The Girl stuck her head in, her face wearing an expression of mild surprise.

"You're awake."

. . .

She was not particularly beautiful. She had a vulnerable nature; an exploitable face which made her ideal for her clientele. She wore years' worth of burdens and heartache on her face, but most of all it rested around her eyes. Her eyes painted a picture of a girl who had seen too much too soon. A jaded hazel that seemed too fragile for her circumstances. It had been about five years since Miss Cestero had taken her off of the streets. She was 21 now, and ready to escape; ready to start again.

There were always regulars. The geezers and the businessmen, the backbone of the industry, really. Then there were tourists; guys who happened to stumble across the little door on that narrow street. Sailors passing through on their travels. New Orleans was a fine spot but it could be overrun by tourists when the season came. She had seen the city in an exposed light, being there year-round, when the seediest parts of it came out to play. It all had its ups and downs, its pros and cons, but when it came right down to it, she was still stuck. Being paraded around next to naked with 20 other girls and then being selected at random according to the John's discretion. Most days it didn't bother her. She would be somewhere else, different things on her mind, in another world. Some days there was a profound hurt that struck her at a moment's notice. Shame, desperation, isolation; a perfect storm of inner torment.

She had liked it at first. The idea of her business being pleasure. What could be better than getting paid to indulge in the world's oldest and greatest pastime? But she soon grew tired and weary; the experience had made her feel old and cynical before her time. It was a problem common in the profession, one too many feigned moans or painfully common terms of endearment. It wore down on the spirit.

She walked in and sat down on the bed, never once taking her eyes off of him. He turned and faced her, dragging down the last bit of his cigarette.

"Name's Frank." He rasped, exhaling and looking for an ashtray.

"Hi, Frank." She said, handing him a clear crystal one off of the nightstand next to the bed. "We thought we'd lost you for a while there. You sat up and got a little better in the middle of the night, so I figured you'd live."

His chest tightened. "L-Lost me? Jesus, did I almost die?"

"Oh, you're fine. It's not the first time something like this has happened." She smiled at him from behind her red lips and gestured for the pack of cigarettes. She was kindly overlooking his violation of Drug Etiquette rule number 1: Never turn blue in someone else's room.

Frank tried to regroup quickly, realizing that he'd overdosed on whatever it was that he took the night before. A cocktail of pills, tequila, and Bourbon Street's World Famous Hand Grenades. Thinking a bit harder he remembered that the pills were crushed and quickly consumed in a bathroom stall, then immediately washed down with the Everclear punch of a Hand Grenade. The rest of the night was a mind-bending haze that could only be described as a glorified Brown Out.

"How long was I like this?" He asked tentatively, and then a bit more forward. "How long was I out?"

She pursed her pretty lips at the question, crossing her ankles and looking up at the ceiling to retrieve the answer. "Ohh…" She started, "Off and on about two days." She placed two cigarettes in her mouth and lit them simultaneously.

"*Jesus Christ!*" He thought to himself. Two days out cold or at least in such a state that he couldn't remember. He tried to recall how he'd even made his way there, but found only haze and confusion. Blacked out links in the chain of his memory.

Handing him a cigarette, she looked at his frustration and horror curiously, her face somewhat sad. Then, after a shallow exhale, she hopped off of the bed and clicked towards the door.

"Wait!" He said quickly, and a bit louder than he meant to. She startled and turned to face him. "Tell me how I got in here. I need to know. Besides, it'd be kinda nice to have someone to talk to."

She cocked her head and looked at him for a brief moment, before shrugging out a casual "ok" and sitting back on the bed. No sooner did her bottom hit the mattress, she popped up and dashed out the door. "Drinks!" She said. "I'll be right back"

She returned quickly with vodka and a glass container of orange juice. "This'll make you feel better." She said, placing the bottles on the nightstand. They stood there looking at each other for a moment, sharing lipstick stained cigarettes under a scratched and faded no-smoking sign high on the wall.

The pale, anonymous taste of the vodka didn't do much for him at first, but he drank deeply from the glass she gave him and sat down on the floor, his back resting on the bed.

She joined him on the floor, bringing the bottles with her and mixed herself a drink.

"So..." She started, locking her fingers around her knees. "What brought you all the way down here to New Orleans?"

"Well," he said, pulling his sport coat on and setting his cigarettes on the floor. "I've been out on the road for a few months now. Going places I've never been before. I had some things happen in the winter... I'm just starting over really."

"What happened? Besides, this isn't a place to start over."

"I don't wanna talk about it right now. It's depressing."

"Aw, c'mon." she nudged, her fingers opening and closing around the bottle.

He looked past her and decided it was time he told *someone*. Why not her?

"This past winter my wife and I were having a baby... There were some complications in the labor and it went on for a long time. A really long time." He stopped and choked, looking at the ceiling and regaining his composure.

"We were trying so hard for so long, and it seemed like things were finally going our way. We had our ups and downs, and the baby thing put a Hell of a strain on our marriage until she finally got pregnant. Then when the day came... For it to all fall apart like that... I just don't know what kind of sign that is."

The girl sat silently stunned. After a few moments passed she asked in a near whisper, "What happened?"

"We lost him shortly after the delivery. I don't think she ever recovered. She was depressed and angry for months afterwards. I...I-" he trailed off and took another drink.

The girl had leaned in so far that their heads were almost

touching. Just inches apart from each other. Her eyes had grown wet and a lump had formed in her throat.

"Oh, my God…" she breathed.

"Then one day, she just shut down. Just stopped talking to me. It was only a matter of time until she gave me the papers. I stayed in the house about a week after she left, but it was too big, too empty. We didn't have the heart to tear down the baby's room, and I couldn't stand seeing that crib anymore. So I started driving. I've just been trying to start over. Find someplace I can rest my head. I don't have the nerve to go back there, and I'm not sure I'll ever have it. I'm shot; just trying to find something to anchor down to. For now, it's the road.

A strong current of silence ran between them. He finished his drink. She lit another pair of cigarettes and handed one to him.

"I know I'm nobody to be givin you advice, and I can't even begin to imagine the hurt you're goin through right now…But I've learned a few things in this life. When you lose something, or someone, you gotta move on."

She furrowed her brow and thought of a gentler phrase.

"Press on. That's the only way to survive. Just keep moving. It's so tough sometimes, and we don't want to leave them behind, but it's the only way. What you don't have, you don't need anymore. It sounds heartless but it's the truth."

As he dragged on his cigarette, his eyes took on a glazed look as he struggled to respond. He understood, but had trouble communicating it. His legs started to go numb and he managed a nod.

Amidst her life lesson she had missed some of his troubling signals. She stared aimlessly into the half empty bottle of vodka . "But I don't think running will fix anything…" As the words were leaving her mouth she looked over at his increasingly baffled face. He made an attempt to stand, and then slumped back against the bed.

"I don't feel so hot…"

Frank's eyes closed slowly as he lost consciousness for the 3rd time that weekend.

. . .

She knew the drugs would soon be out of his system, and the vodka would run its course, but the root of the problem remained. She wondered if there was anything she could do to help him. She could barely help herself. A decision had to be made. That weekend was to be her moment, her time to escape. Buy her way out and start over again. She also knew that for Frank, starting over meant moving on. Away from the madness he had created for himself.

After sitting next to his unconscious body for nearly half an hour, she stood up and clicked across the hall to change clothes. She packed a small bag and untucked the manila envelope from behind her dresser.

Frank awoke to the forward lurch of the 4:05 out of the New Orleans Amtrak station. His ticket was in his lap with a handicap sticker on it and his headache was starting to dissipate. Looking around, he realized where he was and what had happened. The train pulled forward and out of the station towards his home. He tried to wrap his mind around it, why a total stranger…a hooker at that, would try and help him in his hour of need.

Back on Bourbon Street, the girl looked out the window and listened to the bell as the train left the station. She thought about Frank, and the decision she made to stay behind. He had to leave then, even though he couldn't see it. How would she know when it was her time? As the city pulsed and danced beneath her window, she wondered if she was waiting on a moment that would never come.

The Empty Boulevards

"And I called for my father, but my father had died…While you told me fortunes in American Slang"

The hallway was as dark and dank as ever when they came and grabbed him from his cell. The Condemned look up when he heard the clang of the lock turning in his cell door. The bars flew back and the guards rushed in, beating him savagely across the back and ribcage with their batons, kicking and spitting on him and smirking all the while. They finally lifted him to his feet, and as he stumbled to get his balance, one of the guards laid him out with a right cross to his mouth. Grinding the gristle between his teeth and spitting blood, the Condemned got to his hands and knees in an attempt to stand; but before he could, the guards snatched him up and dragged him down the corridor.

The other inmates howled and cheered and booed and hissed as the guards hauled the Condemned down the corridor, his feet dragging behind him. He hadn't eaten in three days and his mind had started to go. His hair had gotten long and greasy and his beard was patchy, dirty and ungroomed. Blood trickled from his mouth into his beard as they came upon the enormous, gray wood and steel double doors. The guards stopped, and straightened themselves up before knocking on the titanic doors with a phony sense of pomp and grandeur. A moment passed and the Condemned was able to look up just in time to hear the painfully loud sound of the bolt being lifted. The doors slowly opened and a fresh, more regal looking pair of guards stood behind it.

The Condemned looked up at his own guards; combed over, greasy hair, yellow-brown teeth, a false sense of entitlement. One of them was a large, fat, slobbering moron who seemed to fancy himself an intimidating, masculine, hero of a man, a sort of Heracles in rags. The other was a lean fellow with a ridiculous, walrus looking moustache. He was the brains of the outfit, if one could assign such a position to two thunderous dolts as these.

The fresh guards stepped forward and slapped the tramps across the backs of their heads, and continued to cuff them until they retreated from the Condemned and hissed back into their insidious underworld. The officers grabbed hold of either side of him and marched forward through the double doors. Light danced from the windows nearly fifty feet above their heads; it was the first time the Condemned had seen in it a month. He had lost all sense of time. What day was it? What month? In that internal inquiry, he realized the dreadful truth. He couldn't remember his own name. Panic flickered across his chest and into his brain, he tried to recall memories before incarceration, something to give him an idea of who he was or what he did. In a miserable turn, when he went into his mind for a memory, he only saw the beatings, the humiliation and the awful food he received whilst behind bars.

A new set of doors opened to a blinding light and a deafening crowd. His was in an arena of some sort, a small one, the size of a middle school gymnasium. The officers pushed him to his knees and through his hair he could see a man in the center of a panel. The voice came over the loudspeaker. "Have you anything to say?" the voice boomed, crashing through the Condemned's head and rattling his insides. He said nothing, mostly because he didn't understand the words; he just felt the force of the volume and the reverb.

Six men stood in front of him, rifles at their sides; a man in the corner whistled, and they popped to and brought the rifles to the ready. Sweat caressed their palms and their hearts thumped a little faster in their chests as the man's hand rose steadily into the air. Six bolts clicked. Jarred awake by the sound, he opened his eyes. As the man's hand dropped, the Condemned screamed, "Tell me who I am!" Six rifles fired as one massive thunderclap, and the Condemned fell to the ground…

• • •

David Patterson shot up in the bed, doused in sweat. It had only been a dream. Another nightmare in a long line. His wife put a hand on his chest and lowered him back in the bed, quieting his heavy breathing and silently reassuring him that everything would be alright. He looked at the clock; it was only 3:16 am. He had to be on a plane in five hours to go home and bury his father.

It had only been a year since he'd been discharged from the Navy. A long, arduous year spent ineffectively trying to transition from HM2 Patterson to "David". The insomnia, the panic attacks, and when he did get to sleep, the vivid nightmares. Every time he closed his eyes the faces of the dead drifted up from the darkness, he saw young men wailing and clawing at hopelessly open wounds, entrails ruptured and exposed to the unforgiving desert sun. Men face down in the dirt, covered in blood. Women and children burned beyond recognition, and anonymous limbs littering the sidewalks after IED's destroyed a marketplace or a school. Sometimes it was too much, sometimes he just wanted it to be over.

He remembered when the visions were at their worst; auditory hallucinations, vivid nightmares, he couldn't eat, and barely slept. One night he sat in his den, shrouded in darkness save for one lamp on the desk, beside it sat his M9 service pistol. He picked it up and removed the clip, leaving just one round in the chamber. His teeth rested on the barrel, the metallic taste of steel on his tongue and one thing on his mind. *It could all be over… just do it, it'd be so easy…* He thought, index finger caressing the trigger, almost teasing it. Closing his eyes he tightened his grip on the butt of the pistol and ripped it from his mouth, disarming the weapon and ejecting the round into the palm of his hand. Placing the round in the center of the desk, he turned off the lamp and went to bed.

"Wake up, babe, we're gonna be late." His wife called to him. David opened his eyes and looked at the clock, it was 6:22, and his wife's suitcases were lined up against the door. He looked over to the other side of the room and saw his duffel bag open, ready for last minute entries. Rising out of the bed, he trudged to the bathroom and washed his face; his reflection told him that he'd slept with the nicotine patch on. He brought the small bag of toiletries into the bedroom and dropped them in the duffel bag with his toothbrush still in his mouth, walking back he saw his wife had laid out the clothes he had hanging up. "Hey June?" He called to his wife, "Where's my watch?" "In the dresser, babe. Top drawer." He opened the drawer and took out the battered old digital watch he'd worn every day in Afghanistan. Staring for only a moment, he put it on his wrist and quickly got dressed. Before his wife made it back in the room he stuffed his emergency backup pack of Camel wides into the bag and zipped it up. "Ready to go?" She asked, sticking her head in the doorway. "Right behind you." He said, shouldering the bag and walking out of the bedroom. He took a last look at the room and shut out the light.

Gazing out the window above Arizona, David realized

he hadn't been home in 8 years. When he went on leave he retreated to the house in Tucson and holed up there. No vacations, no road trips, no surprise visits for his mother on Christmas or Thanksgiving, nothing. He was completely isolated in his fortress at the bottom of the world. He tried to let the turbulence rock him to sleep, but to no avail. Shifting restlessly he leaned his head against the seat and stared up at the ceiling, trying to let his mind wander into sleep. He looked over at June, who slept gently beside him; she never had any problems sleeping. A part of him wanted to resent her for her stability, her unwavering longsuffering, but he could never do it. Landing at Akron/Canton they got off the plane and took a cab to his Father's house.

When they pulled up, his father's car was parked in the driveway and a few cars lined the street. His mother rushed and met them on the lawn, putting her face in his chest and sweeping her boy up in a big bear hug. She stepped back and looked him over, "It's good to see you, son. So good to see you." She said gently. Her voice was faltering, tears welling up in her eyes. He nodded and gave a half-smile; all he could muster at the moment. June stepped forward and put her arms out, and the two women embraced. "I'm so sorry. How you holding up, Esther?" "Thank you for bringing my boy to me." She whispered in June's ear. "I couldn't let him miss this, I'd never forgive myself." Esther smiled, and wiping her eyes, showed them into the house where the family was.

David followed behind them, his mind in a reminiscent haze. He stopped short of the porch and saw the tire and rope still swinging from the tree in the backyard, and he remembered years ago, when he was 9 years old and trying out for quarterback on the midget football team. They would practice for hours, putting the ball through the tire, working on accuracy and footwork, being calm under pressure. *That* last lesson lasted a lifetime. It went on for months, and he was getting better and better under his father's tutelage. He slept with his football, ate with it, the two were inseparable. On the day of the tryouts, the coach's son got the job, David landing second string. He waited until his dad started the car and sobbed the whole way home. In the driveway, his father sighed with his massive shoulders, crouched down and looked him in the eye. "Listen, boy. Life's not fair. But that just means you fight twice as hard the next time." He put his large hands on his son's shoulders and gave him a warm, paternal look that said, "Let's go and work at it again." So David wiped his eyes, grabbed his football and ran into the backyard to practice until the streetlights came on.

The memory came swirling back with a rush of emotion that really let him know what had been lost. But in the pit of his stomach, he felt an emptiness, a void that he had to reconcile, the reason he'd come back. He was annoyed at his inability to emote at such an appropriate time; he scratched his nicotine patch resentfully and walked through the door.

. . .

A small gathering of aunts and uncles, distant cousins and one neighbor greeted David when he entered the kitchen. *Who are these people?* He thought to himself. The faces were familiar if only a bit aged, but they had no meaning to him. These people who hugged him and his wife, who were regurgitating stories of years gone by, the meant nothing, they were strangers. He looked blank and harmlessly into their faces while their mouths rambled away with questions and formalities and condolences. June eased up and locked arms with him, seeming to sense his mind drifting into detachment. She wouldn't let him run; not from this.

His mother called off the swarming relatives to show

the couple their bedroom. The two walked upstairs, to what used to be David's old room, and stood in the doorway. "I'll leave you two for a while" she said, and drifted back downstairs.

· · ·

"You're lucky you never really knew your old man. They don't do anything but let you down."

Suddenly he found himself downstairs in the kitchen, talking to an embittered 2nd cousin (or something) about father-figures. Something actually registered in him, told him to defend his father, to put up a fight. "They may not all be the best, but they teach us huge lessons. Even the bad ones."

"Yeah, like what?"

"Self-reliance: There'll be times that he's not around, Hell, when **no one** is around, and you have to be the man in the situation, take charge. They teach us courage: If you ever had to stick up for your Mother when your old man came home drunk and angry, ready to take out his frustration. They teach us that nobody's perfect, and that sometimes, when we try and do right... we're fighting a losing battle. That's important."

"Sounds like a load-a shit. But I guess I never thought of it that way." The cousin shrugged. "I guess they're gonna be a big part of your life no matter what they do. Might as well learn from it."

"Exactly." David said, and somehow he felt a little better.

His father had never been abusive, wasn't a drunk, and was usually there when he needed him. If anybody was abandoned and mistreated, it was his parents. He started to think about that emptiness, that hollow feeling he had inside when he came back to his old hometown. Then he remembered the look in his father's eyes in those last years before he moved out. That faraway gaze in the evening as he sat on the back porch smoking his pipe and listening to the radio. Sometimes he'd watch him through the kitchen window while he did the dishes. He wondered how a man with a steady job and a family could look so alone.

Wandering through the crowd he overheard some conversations; memories of his dad, old relatives catching up. It was strange that some people only see each other at weddings, funerals, milestone birthday parties, and baptisms. The phrase, "I haven't seen you since Uncle Greg turned 50." Or, "How've you been since Grandma died?" Should never be your standard opener. No friendship survives on discussing how tastefully an old lady's corpse was displayed.

Before he got to the back porch, he heard an older uncle talking to his cousin who'd recently been laid off from the Timken factory, starting a string of bad luck.

"I've known you your whole life, boy. You were born ass first, lived life assed outta luck, and probably gonna die that way." He drawled. "Ain't nothin gonnna change that now. You can try all you want."

The cousin looked at the floor while he was being berated by a craggy, leathery, spitting old man. David nearly said something, but instead turned his head and walked onto the porch where his mother was sitting with her sister and the neighbor.

"Hey, son, how you doin'?" She said gently. He paused for a moment at the question. Taken aback by how such a trivial formality could seem so inappropriate or unnecessary, he ignored the question. "I was just checkin up on you. Hadn't seen you in a few." "I'm just fine, son. Fine." She assured him. "You remember Aunt Sarah and Ms. Catherine don't you?" She turned to them, gesturing, "This is my boy." As if none of the time had ever escaped; like everything was normal.

They greeted each other cordially, and the ladies returned to their conversation, leaving David stranded on the outside of their circle. Sensing her son's discomfort, she turned to him, "You look tired, son. I know you've come a mighty long way. No use in stayin up on account of me. Why don't you go rest a while?" With a knowing look, she gave him an out to go upstairs and escape the flood of people in the house. Leaning down and getting a kiss on the cheek, he turned away from his mother and walked into the house.

· · ·

David sat on the edge of the bed, thinking about the day, and how long it had been since he'd last walked through the house. He scratched his nicotine patch. There was a quiet frustration running through him, wondering why he wasn't feeling what he was "supposed" to at such a crucial time. June rubbed his shoulders and whispered in his ear, "Come to bed, c'mon." He laid down in the bed and stared at the ceiling until June fell quietly back to sleep...

The unit was making its way to the military hospital in Kandahar. Low on fuel, they stopped just outside the city near a shelter. Walking through a row of tents to the entrance, David saw many women, some Afghan and some not, who were scarred and bruised all over their bodies. Some had burns across their face, others used crutches, some were even pregnant. He tried to look straight ahead and avoid the eyes of the victims in the camp, like they were that homeless guy trying to bum a cigarette back home.

They entered the shelter on the first floor, and he watched the Sergeant move to the counter and speak with the man behind it in Arabic. Some of the Marines stayed put, but it was generally understood that they'd be there for a while. He and two other guys walked down a narrow, eggshell colored hallway to some large and open rooms. They weren't carpeted, and there was no air condition, but somehow it was still silently acknowledged that this was the "nice" part of the building. They saw a few women sitting in one of the rooms with a doctor, who after spotting them, said something to the group, and then beckoned them in.

There were many scars and burns and bandages in the room, but the woman who was speaking when they sat down grabbed everyone's attention. She was sitting in the left part of the semi-circle, dressed modestly in an ankle-length skirt, and a loose-fitting top that flared at her wrists to reveal hands aged beyond their years, suggesting she worked with her hands to the point of wear and tear. The skin over her slightly enflamed knuckles was healing from what looked to be a serious scrape. David's eyes worked up to her face as she spoke, and he saw that she had no nose. There were scars around the edge of the place where the nose should be, and her hair was short and uneven in patches on her head.

She had told the group where she came from, and the story of how the Taliban came to take over her village years ago, but generally left her family alone. David's Arabic was very basic and fragmented, so Powell provided a very hushed translation in his ear. She paused for a moment and looked to the Doctor, and then she began to speak.

The Taliban had been on a rampage as of late, and her village was a particular target for their ruthlessness and scorn. They had burned down part of the market, torn the roofs off of the homes of some elderly people, and beaten countless strangers in the middle of the street. One day, a Wednesday, as she recalled, she was walking home after picking up some food from the functioning side of the market when they came bursting into town. She dropped her bags and ran for a hiding spot in an alley. She heard gunfire and shouting for a long time, and when it all quieted down she started to come out from her hiding spot, just as one of the men came around the corner into the alley. She ducked behind some boxes as he relieved himself against the opposite wall. She was absolutely terrified, and to her horror, let out a quiet, strangled, whimper. The man whirled around and looked at the boxes she was hiding behind. Walking around, he called her over to him. When she tried to run, he caught her easily and dragged her by the arm out into the street with the rest of the men in a stolen truck. They laughed and hooped when she came into view, and when she tried to struggle and break free, her captor hauled off and slugged her in the stomach, knocking the wind out of her. He snatched her by the hair and tossed her up into the truck as they drove off.

They took her about 3 miles outside of the village to a small, shack of a house. In the back of the truck she realized that these men were all around 19 or 20 years old, the eldest being 23, if that. Some of them laughed and kicked at her, but most of them just stared quietly. The truck came to a tired and rumbling stop outside the house, the exhaust wheezing as the men piled out. She was pushed out onto the ground, where she tried to run again, but was grabbed by the eldest of the men and carried inside like a piece of furniture.

The inside of the place was dark and dirty, and a light stench hit her nostrils when she was dropped in the basement ("like a locker room with no indoor plumbing" was Powell's own analogy). There were no questions asked, and only a moment's hesitation before they pounced on her as a mob. They beat her savagely and cut her clothes off as they cursed her and her village; her family. For the next day and a half she was battered, raped, and sodomized repeatedly before they chopped her hair off. The next morning she was loaded into the truck, and dropped off, naked and bleeding, in front of the market in her village. A week later, some of the men in the village found her and cut off her nose for shaming their community.

The woman on the far right began to weep.

Everyone in the room sat silent. Stunned by the horrifying story of cruelty, and amazed that she had survived to tell the tale. David looked over his shoulder to see Martinez stick his head in the doorway, the Humvee was fueled up and ready to go. David gestured for Powell and Thomas to leave with him, and they quietly stood to their feet. Powell looked back at the Doctor, "Shokran" he said softly, and taking one last look at the woman, walked out of the room and down the corridor. No one in that room was ever quite the same after hearing that story.

Powell was killed the next week by an IED.

• • •

David woke up in the bed, sweating and breathing heavily. The dreams were so vivid; they took so much energy out of him. He swung his feet out of the bed and onto the floor and rested his head in his hands, elbows on his knees. Taking a moment to collect himself, he quietly stood up, so he didn't wake June, and shuffled over to his duffel bag. Kneeling down, he slowly unzipped it and removed his emergency reserve pack of Camel Wides and his lucky Zippo. He cursed himself a second for falling off the wagon, but he decided he needed a cigarette now more than ever.

He eased the sliding screen door open and walked out onto the porch. He looked around for a moment, and then tentatively sat down in his father's chair. Lighting his cigarette, he took a long, much needed drag and exhaled through his nose and teeth in relief. He thought about his father, and what he must've been feeling in those last years before his son moved out. He wondered if he had felt the same isolation, the same loneliness, the same emptiness that plagued him now. That faraway look in his eyes seemed to say so much in his head, but was so hard to explain when he thought it out. He wondered if his father had dreams. Dreams that he had to put aside to raise his family. Then in the twilight of his years, he looked back on his life, or looked out into the night and thought about what might have been. He wondered if he was bitter.

David thought about the funeral in the morning. He looked at his watch. 4:25 a.m. It was only in a few hours. He ashed his third cigarette and stood up. He was going to face his family. He was going to be there and be strong for his mother. He was going to say goodbye to his father, even though they never had a proper conversation as adults. These things just seemed to come to him in his father's chair; he knew what he had to do. He put the cigarette out and put the butt in a beer can that sat on the floor between the door and the chairs. Easing through the slide door once again, he walked lightly to his room and put his cigarettes away in his duffel bag. He slid back into bed next to June, who stirred a little, but stayed asleep. He kissed her forehead, laid back down and slept until it was time to wake up for the funeral.

. . .

That afternoon he said goodbye to his mother, who hugged and kissed him over and over, insisting "It may be another 8 years til I see you again, boy! Let your mother love you!"

He smiled and embraced her in the driveway one last time, and then June said her goodbyes. They got in his father's car and backed out into the street, Esther waving and grinning, seeing them off. David was amazed that a woman in such a state of grief could be so warm and hospitable to everyone. "Of course she's heartbroken… But when she lost a husband, she got her son back, and that makes things a little easier." June said, seeming to read his mind. He looked warmly over at his wife and she took his hand in hers, and they drove off to the airport to fly back that night.

One Year Later . . .

As the sun set behind the trees, he waded deeper into the river. The burst of color and light splashed across the sky and warmed him as he closed his eyes and went under. Beneath the surface, he tried to invent a reason why he never knew his father, and why he'd waited until it was too late to find solace and meaning in the relationship. Too late in the day. Darkness had fallen on any chance of mutual understanding between the two, despite being haunted by the same old ghosts. Standing to his feet, he wiped his face and looked across the bank as if he was going to be given some convenient spiritual sign or epiphany. He groped for something profound to say or think. Finding nothing, he walked ashore. He laid down in an open spot next to his shoes and socks where the sun could dry him as it was setting. It was getting even cooler at night now; fall was coming. He stood up, dry enough now to get in his car. Taking one last look at the river, he walked through the woods to the road.

Driving home, he felt an old emptiness creep up inside him. Not quite sadness, but that raw, hollow feeling that he couldn't explain. Since his father's funeral he'd learned to suppress it. To fight it, but every so often it would take hold of him with the strength and purpose to drag him down. He opened the front door to find June asleep at the kitchen table with the light on. She awoke with the sound of the door closing and quietly rushed over to him. Noticing that his hair and clothes were still damp, she gave him a look of disquiet and embraced him in the doorway. He gestured with his eyes upstairs and she nodded; taking his hand, they ascended the stairs and cracked open the door to their son's room. His crib was in the center of the room, a little solar system above it, the walls were recently painted but the old curtains were still up. The boy slept silently, balling up his little fists and moving slightly enough to construe he was dreaming.

"It's important, these little moments." She said, reaching up her hand and rubbing his chin. "A father can do a lot for a boy when he's small. So when he becomes a man, he doesn't have far to look for guidance. Boys need that father figure so they don't get lost along the way."

"Yeah." He said, lifting his chin from her shoulder, "It'd be nice."